Ethan bent in and brought his mouth to Holly's. Only it wasn't a feather-soft dinner kiss, meant to fool his aunt. No, his unexpected lips were bold. And hot. And they smashed against hers.

Their insistence didn't let her pull away. Instead, she swirled inside. Got lost in the moment. Let it go on several beats too many.

Until she could finally separate herself from him.

Holly feared everyone at the table could hear her heart pounding outside her chest.

Ethan looked as shocked as she felt. But after a moment he picked up his fork and resumed eating. Following his lead, she did the same.

Fortunately neither Louise nor Fernando had noticed anything strange. Holly and Ethan were engaged, after all. Why *wouldn't* they spontaneously kiss?

But he wasn't helping her any with a kiss like that. Let that be a warning to her.

Dear Reader,

I'm so excited that my writing journey has brought me to you. I've been scribing for as long as I can remember—from the silly skits of a child, to a teenager's angst-ridden diaries and more mature stories as an adult. Somewhere along my way I landed as a journalist. Hundreds of non-fiction articles and a couple of awards later, I am now living my lifelong dream of writing romantic fiction!

With my debut novel for Mills & Boon I invite you to follow Holly and Ethan's rocky road to love. While it's a fast and fun trip, they meet as two strangers so emotionally wounded they can't believe that happily-ever-after might be in their futures.

The idea struck me that a million dramas are unfolding in New York City at any given moment. So I chose *those* two people in *that* second-floor window, forced together by a stormy night. The last thing either of them wants is to get tangled up in someone else's life, yet they discover mutually beneficial reasons to stay.

Ethan has been in my head for a long time. I love a complicated hero like him, who is sophisticated, successful and noble, but whose damage peeks out from behind his soulful eyes. And Holly is like any of us who are determined to rise up from the ashes and turn our hopes into reality.

I can't wait to share more romantic voyages with you. Let me know what you think about Holly and Ethan!

Andrea x

HER NEW YORK
BILLIONAIRE

BY
ANDREA BOLTER

First Published in Great Britain 2017
By Mills & Boon, an imprint of HarperCollins*Publishers*
1 London Bridge Street, London, SE1 9GF

© 2017 Andrea Bolter

ISBN: 978-0-263-06974-7

Our policy is to use papers that are natural, renewable and recyclable
products and made from wood grown in sustainable forests. The logging
and manufacturing processes conform to the legal environmental
regulations of the country of origin.

Printed and bound in Great Britain
by CPI Antony Rowe, Chippenham, Wiltshire

Andrea Bolter has always been fascinated by matters of the heart. In fact she's the one her girlfriends turn to for advice with their love-lives. A city mouse, she lives in Los Angeles with her husband and daughter. She loves travel, rock 'n' roll, sitting at cafés, and watching romantic comedies she's already seen a hundred times. Say hi at andreabolter.com.

Her New York Billionaire
is Andrea Bolter's debut title for Mills & Boon.

Visit the Author Profile page at millsandboon.co.uk.

For Alex

CHAPTER ONE

"WHY IS YOUR face blue?"

Holly froze in shock. She had just opened the door to the apartment she'd expected to find empty. But instead of flicking on the lights in a vacant living room she'd walked in on lamps already blazing. And a shirtless man sitting in the center of the sofa. Reading a newspaper. A gorgeous brown-haired shirtless man was reading a newspaper.

"Why is your face blue?" he repeated. Broad shoulders peeked out over the newspaper he was holding.

Why is your face blue? Holly heard the individual words but couldn't put them together to understand them as a question. She could hardly get over the fact that there was a man in the apartment, let alone make sense of the sounds coming from his mouth.

She checked the keys in her hand. Perhaps she was somehow in the wrong place.

And then she saw.

Her hands were blue. Cobalt Blue Two Eleven, to be exact. She'd know that color anywhere. It was one of her favorites.

It suddenly made sense. Just a few minutes ago she'd ducked out of the rain and under the front awning of the building to rifle through her duffel bag for the piece of paper that confirmed the address. The duffel held paint tubes and brushes, paperwork, clothes and heaven knew what else. The cap must have come off her Cobalt Two Eleven.

And she must have touched her face with paint-covered hands.

"What are you doing here?" Holly asked the shirtless man.

"This apartment belongs to my company."

He lowered his newspaper, folded it matter-of-factly and laid it beside him. Giving Holly a full view of his long, lean torso that led down to the plaid pajama bottoms covering the lower half of his body.

"What is it that *you* are doing here?"

The lump that had balled in Holly's throat delayed her response. She hadn't seen a half-naked man in a very long time. And she hadn't seen a man who looked like he did while he was busy being half-naked in...well, possibly ever.

"I'm staying here," she answered.

It had been a grueling journey, and the last thing she'd expected was to have to reckon with someone once she got here.

She blinked her eyes hard to pull herself together and tried not to panic. "I was told I could use this apartment."

"That must have been a mistake."

Mistake? What was this man talking about?

"I've just arrived from Florida. My brother, Vince, works in the Miami office of Benton Worldwide Properties. This is one of the apartments they keep for visitors to New York."

"That is correct."

"Vince arranged for me to stay here. He confirmed it last week. And he called again yesterday to Benton Boston headquarters."

"I am Ethan Benton, Vice President of Benton Worldwide. As you can see from my…" he gestured down his chest "…state of undress, *I* am staying here at the moment."

"Okay, well, I'm Holly Motta and I was counting on using this apartment. See?" She shook the blue-painted keys. "The Boston office left the keys in my name with the doorman downstairs."

"I apologize for the mistake. I have just arrived tonight myself. In the morning I will look into who is responsible for this egregious error and have their head lopped off."

The left corner of his mouth hitched up a bit.

Ethan Benton and his bare chest sat on a black leather sofa. Matching armchairs faced opposite, separated by a modern glass coffee table. The furnishings were spare. Two large framed photos were the only adornments on the wall. Both black and white, one was of a potted orchid and the other a maple tree.

Bland as a plain piece of toast. A typical corporate apartment, Holly guessed, having never been in one before. Elegant, yet all business. With no personal touches.

It was hardly the type of place where a beautiful shirtless man should be reading a newspaper. Not at all the kind of place where one brown curl of hair would fall in front of that man's forehead as if it were no big deal. As if that wasn't the most charming thing that a wet and exhausted young woman from Fort Pierce, Florida could imagine.

"Again, so sorry for the miscommunication," said the man that curl belonged to, "but you are going to have to leave. I will have the doorman hail you a taxi."

"Not so fast."

Holly snapped out of her fascination with his hair. She stomped over to one of the chairs opposite the sofa. Keeping her blue hands in the air, so as not to get paint anywhere, she lowered herself down.

"If your corporate office didn't have you scheduled to stay here, maybe it's *you* who should leave."

The corner of his mouth ticked up again—which was either cute or annoying. Holly wasn't sure yet.

"Obviously I am not going to leave my company's apartment."

Holly couldn't believe this was happening. This morning she had taken a bus from Fort Pierce to West Palm Beach airport. Then her flight to Newark, New Jersey had been delayed. When it had finally landed she'd taken another bus to the Port Authority terminal in Manhattan. It had been raining and dark by then, and there had hardly been a taxi to be had. She'd got drenched flagging one down. The cab brought her to this address on the Upper East Side.

And now—same as always, just when she was trying to do something for herself—someone else's need was somehow one-upping hers.

"What am I supposed to do?"

"I would suggest you go to a hotel."

Hotels in New York were expensive. Holly had been saving money for months to make a go of it when she got here. She couldn't use up any of her funds on a hotel stay.

"I can't afford it."

Ethan fixed a strangely searching stare on her.

While he assessed her Holly's eyes followed his long fingers as they casually traced the taut muscles of his chest down and then back up again. Down. And up. Down. And up.

After seemingly giving it some thought, he reasoned, "You must know people in New York that you can stay with?"

"No. I don't know anyone here. I came here to…"

Holly stopped herself. This man was a total stranger. She shouldn't be telling him anything about her life. He didn't need to know about her ex-husband, Ricky the Rat, her crazy mom, or any of it.

Maybe all that chaos was behind her now. Maybe the whole world was at her feet. Or maybe there were more hard times ahead.

Holly didn't know. But she was going to find out.

Hard rain continued to pelt against the window.

An unwelcome tear dropped its way out of her eye. When she instinctively reached up to brush it away before Ethan noticed she found Cobalt Two Eleven was smeared on the back of her hand as well.

"Are you *crying*?" Ethan asked, as if he were observing a revolutionary scientific function.

"I'm not crying," Holly denied. "It's been a long day."

"Perhaps you would like use the bathroom to wash up," Ethan offered. He pointed behind him. "It is the door on the right."

"Thank you." Holly hoisted herself up without touching anything, and made her way past Ethan and his curl of hair. "By the way—I'm not leaving."

Behind the sofa was a small dining table made of glass and steel like the coffee table. Four orange leather dining chairs provided a much-needed pop of color. Beyond that was a teeny kitchen.

Her brother had told her it was a very compact one-bedroom apartment. It would do quite fine. This was to be a temporary stepping stone for Holly. Either she was in New York to stay or it was merely a transition to somewhere else. Only time would tell.

She found her way into the marble-appointed bathroom and tapped the door closed with her boot. Made a mental commitment to also slam the door shut on her intense immediate attraction to Ethan Benton...astoundingly handsome, half-naked. Although it took her a stubborn minute to stop wondering what it might be like to lay her cheek against the firmness of one of those brawny shoulders.

Oh, no! She caught her reflection in the mirror above

the sink. It was so much worse than she could have envisioned. She had Cobalt Two Eleven streaked across her
face in horizontal stripes. Like a tribal warrior. Her black
bangs were plastered to her forehead in sweaty points.
She was a scary mess. What must this man think of her?

Not wanting to get anything dirty, she used her elbow to
start the faucet. With both hands under the running water,
she saw color begin swirling down the drain. She rubbed
her hands together until enough paint was removed that
she could adjust the tap to make the water hotter and pick
up the pristine bar of white soap.

Eventually her hands were scoured clean—save for a little residual blue around the cuticles and under the nails. As
usual. She reached for the fluffy towel hanging on the rack.

Next, Holly wanted to get her jacket off before she tack-
led washing her face. She unzipped the sleek and stylish
black leather jacket she had bought at the shopping mall
in Fort Pierce yesterday. With Florida's mild climate, there
hadn't been a lot of selection, but she'd needed something
warm for New York. When she'd seen it, she'd known it
was the one for her.

Ricky the Rat would have hated it. He'd have said it
was highfalutin'. Yeah, well, falute *this*! Decisions were
going to be made *by* her, *for* her from now on. Not based
on what other people wanted or thought.

After her face was scrubbed she towel-dried her bangs
and peeled off her ponytail band. Fluffed out the dark hair
that had grown far past her shoulders. With the longer hair,
she realized she already had a new look. New hair. New
jacket. New city. She was ready for a new life.

Giving a yank on her tee shirt and a tug on her jeans,
she was more than a little concerned about how she'd look
to Ethan when she went back into the living room. Which
was, of course, completely ridiculous because she didn't
even know him.

* * *

My, my, but Holly Motta cleaned up well. Distracted by the blue paint on her face, Ethan hadn't noticed the other blue. The crystal color of her eyes. How they played against her lush jet-black hair.

As soon as she returned from the bathroom a rush of energy swept through the living room. He didn't know what kind of magic she held, but it wasn't like anything he had been in the same space with before.

All he could mutter was, "Better?"

It wasn't really a question.

He was glad he had nabbed a tee shirt from the bedroom, although he was still barefoot.

"Yes, thanks." She slid past him to her luggage, still at the front door.

He reached for his computer tablet and tapped the screen. Best to get Holly out of the apartment right now. For starters, he had no idea who she was. Ethan knew firsthand that there were all sorts of liars and scammers in this world, no matter how innocent they might look. He had his family's company to protect. The company that he was to run.

As soon as he could get his aunt Louise to retire.

As if a heart attack hadn't been enough, his beloved aunt was now losing her balance and mobility due to a rare neurological disorder that caused lack of feeling in her feet. Benton Worldwide's annual shareholders' gala was this Saturday. Ethan hoped Aunt Louise didn't have any bruises on her face from the fall he'd heard she'd taken last week.

Ethan owed everything to Aunt Louise and to Uncle Melvin, who had passed away five years ago. Without them he would just have been an abandoned child with no one to guide him toward a future.

His aunt had only one final request before she retired from the company that she, Uncle Mel and Ethan's late father had spent fifty years growing into an empire. She wanted to be sure that Ethan was settled in all areas of his life. Then she'd feel that everything was in its right place before she stepped down and let him take over. One last component to the family plan.

Ethan had lied to his aunt by claiming that he'd found what she wanted him to have. But he hadn't. So he had a lot to take care of in the next few days.

His temples pulsed as he thought about it all. Commotion was not an option. This exhilarating woman who had blown into the apartment needed to leave immediately. Not to mention the fact that there was something far too alluring about her that he had to get away from. Fast.

On top of it all he had a conference call in a few minutes that he still had to prepare for.

But with a few swipes across the tablet's screen he confirmed that all the Benton properties in New York were occupied.

Holly slung her jacket on the coat rack by the door and sat down on the floor. After pulling off one, then the other, she tossed her boots to the side. Ethan was mesmerized by her arms as they rummaged through her bag. She seemed to be made up only of elongated loose limbs that bent freely in every direction. Lanky. Gangly, even.

Downright adorable.

Nothing about Holly was at all like the rigid, hoity-toity blondes he usually kept company with. Women who were all wrong for him. Since he wasn't looking for someone right, that didn't matter. It kept his aunt happy to see him dating. But, of course, now he had told Aunt Louise that was all coming to an end. And he had a plan as to how to cover that lie.

Under her boots, Holly was wearing one red sock and one striped. She rolled those off and wiggled her toes. "That feels good…" She sighed, as if to herself.

Ethan's mouth quirked. "Miss Motta, please do not make yourself at home."

"I have nowhere else to go."

Holly death-stared him right in the face, putting on her best tough guy act. In reality she looked terrified that he was going to throw her out. She'd already been in tears before she washed up.

"Can't *you* be the one to leave?"

His stern expression melted a bit. What was he going to do? Toss her out into the cold rain?

She said she didn't know anyone in New York that she could stay with. Funny, but he didn't either. There were dozens—hundreds—of colleagues and workers in the city, connected with various Benton projects. Yet no one he'd call late on a rainy night to see if they had a sofa or guest room he could use.

Ridiculous. He'd sooner go back to the airport and sleep on his private jet.

He could pay for Holly's hotel room. Or he supposed he himself could go to a hotel. But—good heavens. He'd been in flight all day, had already unpacked and undressed here. Why on earth should he leave his own property?

"I do not suppose it will do for either of us to try to find other accommodation at this late hour."

"What's your plan, then?"

Ethan always had a plan. His life was structured around plans. He was about to embark on his biggest yet—moving Aunt Louise into retirement and taking the CEO seat.

"We will both spend the night here."

"Oh, no, I couldn't. I'm sure you're a very nice per—"

"I assure you, Miss Motta, I have no motive other than getting a peaceful night's rest. You will sleep in the bedroom and I will make do out here." He gestured toward the sofa.

"I need to think about that. That doesn't seem right.

Maybe I should call my brother. Let me just get my things straightened out." Holly returned to her task of sorting out her duffel bag, quarantining paint-stained items in a plastic bag.

She didn't look up at him until she lifted out a pair of white socks. They were splattered with the same blue that had been disguising her lovely face. "Occupational hazard."

"You are a painter, I take it?"

"Yup."

"And you have come to New York to pursue fame and fortune?"

"Ha! That would be nice. Who wouldn't want their work to hang in a museum or a gallery here...?"

"I sense there is a *but* at the end of that."

"I've been making money doing large pieces and collections for corporate properties."

"Office art, lobby art, art for furnished apartments?"

Ethan was well aware of that kind of work. He'd spent many hours with interior designers making decisions about the art at Benton developments all over the world.

"Indeed, the right pieces are vitally important to a unified decor. They announce a mood."

"A point of view," Holly chimed in.

"It sets the tone." He pointed at the two black and white nature photos on the wall. "Those, for example."

"Dull."

"Safe."

"Yawn."

They both laughed in agreement. A sizzle passed between them. It was so real Ethan was sure he saw smoke.

How alive Holly was. The type of person who said exactly what she thought. A bit like Aunt Louise. And nothing at all like most of the women he knew.

He flashed on a possibility.

Then quickly thought better of it.

"My aunt's new husband selected this apartment. He frequently comes down from Boston."

Ethan rolled his eyes. Fernando Layne was no favorite of his. Definitely no substitute for Uncle Mel. Fernando was a plaything for Aunt Louise. Ethan tolerated him.

"I will remodel this property while I am in New York. Perhaps you can advise me?"

What a stupid thing to say. He was never going see Holly again past this awkward evening interlude. An unfamiliar sense of disappointment came over him.

He generally steered clear of his feelings. When they did arrive they were usually of the painful variety and proved too confusing.

"Do you want to look at my website?" Holly gestured to the tablet he still had in his hand.

"I am sorry to be rude but I have a phone meeting in five minutes. I need to prepare."

"At this time of night?"

"I am expecting a call from Tokyo, if you must know." He also wasn't used to explaining himself to anyone. "I will take it in the bedroom," he declared.

Then he picked up a roll of architectural blueprints from the desk and marched down the hall, perturbed in twenty different ways.

Ten o'clock on a rainy New York night.

Holly had left Fort Pierce at eight that morning.

Hungry and tired, she absentmindedly ran her hand along the sofa where Ethan had been sitting when she came in. The leather still held his warmth.

She probably should have been afraid when she'd opened the door to find a total stranger in the apartment. Yet she hadn't felt the slightest inkling of fear. She'd felt ticked off, maybe. Or something else entirely.

It might have something to do with the fact that Ethan Benton looked less like a serial killer than he did the lord of a countryside manor. With his imposing height and lean muscles and that stunning wavy brown hair that had a touch of red flecked in it.

His tone was bossy, but she supposed it must have been quite a shock for him that a woman with a blue face, a tattered duffel bag and a squeaky-wheeled suitcase had just barged into the apartment he'd thought he had to himself.

Now she was trapped here with him unless she was willing to face the stormy night. The man—who may or may not have a British accent—definitely had the most soulful eyes she had ever seen. The man who was now in the next room, conducting business halfway around the world.

New York was getting off to a rollicking start.

Would he be angry with her if she checked to see if there was anything to eat? Should she care, given that this apartment was supposed to be *hers*?

A rumbling stomach propelled her to the kitchen. She'd picked at snacks all day, but had not had a proper meal. On the counter lay one basket of fruit, and another of breads and bagels. The refrigerator held beer, milk, eggs and cheese.

Had this food been purchased for her arrival as a hospitality custom? Or was it Ethan's? Or did it belong to his aunt's husband, who Ethan had said used this apartment frequently?

The sight of the food rendered Holly too hungry to care. Being hungry was a unique ache that she had experience with. Surely Ethan wouldn't mind if she took one shiny red apple.

She hoisted herself up to sit on the countertop. Let her legs and bare feet dangle. Smiled remembering the apple's symbolism here in New York. Like so many others, she was here to take her bite. With one satisfying chomp after the next, her mind wandered about what might be.

"Miss Motta!" Ethan looked startled to find her sitting on the kitchen counter after he finished his call. "Must you always make yourself so…so *comfortable*?"

Holly shrugged her shoulders and slid off the counter-top. *Whatever*. If her sitting on the counter was a big deal to him, she wouldn't do it.

She jutted out her chin. "I bet you haven't eaten."

"Not since early this afternoon on the flight," he confessed. "Is there food?"

"Looks like there's eggs and some things for breakfast."

"We will have something delivered."

"Sounds good to me."

"What would you like?"

"You know what? I haven't been to New York in years. Want to get some famous New York pizza?"

"Pizza it is." He swiped on his tablet. "Yes, Giuseppe's. I ordered from there quite a bit when I was last in New York, working on a project. What type of pizza do you like?"

It was nice of him to let her choose. This man was a bundle of contradictions. Scolding one minute, courteous in the next.

"Everything," she answered, without having to think twice.

"Everything?"

"You know—pepperoni, sausage, salami, mushrooms, onions, peppers, olives. The whole shebang."

"Everything…" he repeated. "Why not?"

"I'll pay for my half."

His mouth twitched.

"Twenty minutes," he read out the online confirmation. She eyed the kitchen clock.

"I guess I'm staying tonight." She crunched on her big apple.

A bolt of lightning struck, flashing bright light through the window.

CHAPTER TWO

ETHAN HAD A peculiar urge. The minute he'd said he'd sleep on the sofa tonight he'd wanted to lie down on the bed with Holly. Not to get under the covers. Just to lie on the bed with her. He wanted to relax. To hold her body against his. Caress her hair. Find out if those ebony locks were as silky as they looked.

Huh. A woman he had never met before, who had charged into his apartment and refused to leave. He had no idea who she really was or what she was doing here.

Yet he wanted to hold her.

The thought had interrupted his phone call several times.

He wasn't going mad. He'd just been working too hard. That was it. It had already been a long evening.

From the moment his flight had landed it had been one thing or another. He'd managed to sort out some of the details for the shareholders' gala. Many more remained. He'd heard there were construction delays on the low-income housing development in the Bronx that was so dear to his heart. He'd talked to a few people at the Boston headquarters to see how Aunt Louise was doing after the fall she'd taken. The news was not good. Then he'd worked on trying to resolve problems with a building permit in Detroit.

It had only been about an hour ago that Ethan had

changed into pajama bottoms and quieted down to read the newspaper. Before Holly had arrived, with the sparkling blue eyes and the creamy skin he now couldn't take his gaze off.

"While we're waiting for the pizza would it be okay if I took a shower?" she asked.

It would be okay if I took it with you.

Ethan surprised himself with the thought he didn't voice. He settled for, "Go right ahead."

Ethan did not like the way warmth resonated from Holly's body when she passed by him en route to the shower. Did not like it a bit because it stirred sensations low within him. Fierce sensations. *Urgent.*

The bathroom door shut with the quick smack that only happened when you closed it with a foot. Did she *always* shut doors with her feet?

His tongue flicked at his upper lip when he heard the sound of the shower. He couldn't help but imagine which article of clothing Holly was removing first. What each long limb might look like uncovered. Her torso was straight, rather than especially curvy, and he envisioned the smooth plain of her back. When he started to imagine what her… Well, he begged his brain to move to a different topic. No easy task.

Normally Ethan maintained a controlled world, without surprises. A world that allowed him to keep the upper hand. Maneuver as he saw fit. Because he was usually right.

Mushroom pizza, for heaven's sake.

A thirty-four-year-old man knew his own ways. Protected his orbit. Holly seemed to tip the universe off-kilter. Made the earth spin off its axis.

He preferred his pizza with only mushrooms on it!

She had to be stopped.

Yet he hadn't the heart to force her out on the street—

especially given the time of night. He didn't doubt that she was capable of fending for herself. But he didn't want her to.

That insane idea glimmered again. He needed to get it out of his head.

Ethan had too much to think about already. He was in a bind. Aunt Louise needed to retire. She'd had a distinguished career, and Ethan wanted her to go out on top. Concern was growing that she would sustain a fall in public. That word would spread. That people might remember her as a woman who had stayed on past her prime. That she was doddering, weak, bruised... All things that Louise Benton was most certainly not.

His aunt and his Uncle Melvin—his father's brother—had taken Ethan in as their own when he was nine years old. Now the time had come for the roles to be reversed. Ethan needed to make sure his decisions were in his aunt's best interests. His father would have told him to. Uncle Mel would have counted on him. It was the very least he could do.

But Aunt Louise had that one condition before she stepped down and moved from frigid Boston to the sunny compound in Barbados they'd had built for just that purpose. She wanted to know that Ethan would run their global business with a stable home life as a foundation.

Even though she and Uncle Mel hadn't been able to have children of their own, they'd experienced the joys and the heartaches of parenting through Ethan. In turn, his aunt wanted *him* to know the profound love of a parent for a child. And the united love and partnership that only came with decades of a shared life.

Aunt Louise would retire once Ethan was engaged to be married.

And because he'd become so alarmed about his aunt's

escalating health problems, and his responsibility to guard her reputation, Ethan had lied to her.

"You always say that deep down in your gut you know when something is right," Ethan had said, twisting his aunt's advice when he'd given her the news that he had met the soul mate he would wed.

Trouble was, Ethan had no such fiancée. Nor would he ever.

That was why he'd come to back to the States a few days ahead of the shareholders' gala. Tomorrow he was having lunch with the woman he planned to marry. In name only, of course.

He'd found a beautiful actress who'd be a suitable bride-to-be. This was New York, after all. There was hardly a better place to find a performer capable of pulling off this charade. He clicked on his tablet to the talent agency website where he'd located Penelope Perkins, an educated and sophisticated blonde with a stately neck.

It was a simple matter, really, in Ethan's mind. He'd chosen the actress and scheduled a meeting with her under the guise of hiring her for a promotional campaign for his company. If he found her to be acceptable and unencumbered he'd have her thoroughly investigated by Benton Worldwide's Head of Security, Chip Foley.

While Chip was completing a background check and every other kind of probe there was, Ethan and his stand-in fiancée would get to know each other and create a history for their relationship. Their engagement would be announced at the gala.

Penelope would also sign numerous non-disclosure and confidentiality agreements. She'd understand that if she were ever to reveal the arrangement she would be sued. Benton lawyers played hardball. They never lost their cases.

For her services, this performer would be paid generously.

It was a solid plan.

"Clean at last." Holly emerged from the bathroom while towel-drying her hair. A fresh tee shirt and sweatpants made her feel cozy after the day's journey. "Traveling makes you so grimy, you know?"

"Yes. I showered on the plane before arrival," Ethan agreed.

"You showered on the plane? How does someone shower on a plane?"

"I have a corporate jet. It does have a number of creature comforts."

Holly whistled. Highfalutin'. "I haven't flown that many times in my life. I'm still excited to get free soda and peanuts."

"Yes, well…perhaps you would enjoy all the amenities on private planes."

She tilted her head to one side and squeezed a little more moisture from the tips of her hair onto the plush towel. Sure, she'd like to be on a private plane, with a shower and enough room for her legs not to feel cramped into a ninety-degree position the entire flight. But that wasn't something that was ever going to happen, so she didn't see any point in discussing it.

"You have a little bit of an accent. And a kind of formal way of talking." Holly had a sometimes bad habit of blurting aloud everything that came into her mind. She called 'em as she saw 'em. "Are you American, or what?"

That left side of his mouth quivered up again in the start of a smile. "Boston-born. Oxford-educated. I would be the complete cliché of an entitled rich boy save for the fact that my father died when I was nine and I was raised by my aunt and uncle."

"What about your mother?"

The landline phone on the desk rang. Ethan turned to answer it. "Thank you. Please send him up." He headed toward the door. "Our pizza is here."

With his back to her, Holly was able to take in the full height of his slim, hard build. Probably about six foot three. Much taller than she was, and she always felt like a giant rag doll.

Ethan moved with effortless authority and confidence. Of course this was a man who showered on planes. This was a man who had been born to shower on planes.

Speaking of showers…it had been weird to shower in the apartment with him there. She knew there was no way he was an axe murderer who was going to hack her to bits. But she couldn't be a hundred percent sure that he was a gentleman who wasn't going to come into the bathroom while she was undressed.

A devilish thrill shot through her at the thought that he might have.

Attraction to a man during her first evening in New York was not on her itinerary. Especially not a man who had put all her plans in jeopardy.

She'd just have to make it through the night. In the morning her brother would help straighten things out about the apartment.

Staying here for a few weeks was meant to be the leg-up that she desperately needed. It would buy her time to find work and decide whether New York was where she should be. It had been two years since she'd kicked out Ricky the Rat. Two years was enough time to move on and move forward.

It was her brother, Vince, who had finally convinced her to take a chance. To take a risk. To take something for her own.

Maybe someday a man would fit into the picture. Not any time soon. She needed to concentrate on herself.

"Join me." Ethan gestured for her to come sit on the sofa after the delivery. He laid the pizza down on the coffee table, then dashed into the kitchen, returning with two plates, a stack of napkins and two bottles. "Will you have a beer?"

She took one from him and popped the cap with a satisfying twist.

As they sat down beside each other Holly winced involuntarily and moved away a bit. Being close to him felt scary. Strange. Strangely great...

He noticed her sudden stiffness. "I do not bite."

Pity. She held back a laugh. It wasn't fear that he'd bite that was bothering her. It might have been fear that he wouldn't.

Ethan flipped open the box and a meaty, cheesy, tomatoey aroma wafted up to their noses.

"I do not believe I have ever seen a pizza with this many ingredients on it."

As if performing a delicate procedure, he used two hands to lift one hefty slice onto a plate and handed it to Holly. Then he served himself.

"Ah..."

They groaned in unison as the first bites slid down their tongues. Unable even to speak, they each quickly devoured their slices.

Holly was the first to reach for a second. Then she sat back on the sofa and put her bare feet up on the coffee table.

"'Everything' is now officially my favorite pizza topping," Ethan confirmed, after taking another slice.

Observing Holly stretched out and seemingly comfortable, he did the same. His leaned back against the sofa.

Tentatively he extended one leg and then the other onto the coffee table, and crossed them just as Holly had hers.

And there they sat, both barefoot, eating pizza, as if they had known each other for eons rather than minutes.

She thought of something to ask. "Where did you fly in from?"

"Dubai. Before that I was in Stockholm. I have been out of the country for a month."

"Where do you live?"

"I keep a small apartment in Boston, near our headquarters. Although I travel most of the time."

"Your company has properties all over the world?"

He nodded and washed down his pizza with a sip of beer. "Yes. Some we build. Some we buy and refurbish. In the last couple of years I have been spending a lot of my time on affordable housing for low-income buyers."

"Vince told me about the development you built in Overtown. He said he was so proud to have been part of a project helping people in one of Miami's neediest areas."

That left side of Ethan's mouth rose up again, but this time it continued until the right side lifted to join it in one full-on heart-melting smile.

Holly almost choked on her pizza. She thought a person might enjoy looking at that smile for the rest of her life.

"After my aunt retires I plan to turn most of Benton's focus toward housing for homeless or low-income families."

"When will she retire?"

Ethan sized Holly up in a gaze that went from the tip of her head down to her toes. As if he were taking her all in. Measuring her for something.

When she couldn't stand the moment any longer she reached for another piece of pizza and pressed, "Does your aunt *want* to retire?"

Holly watched his concentration return to the conversation at hand.

"I think she must, whether she wants to or not. She has peripheral neuropathy. It is a rare inherited condition. She's starting to lose some of her faculties."

"I'm sorry."

"I am, too. She is a wonderful woman."

"She's lucky to have you looking out for her wellbeing." Holly didn't think anyone would ever care about *her* that much.

"I would like to see her relaxing in Barbados. Swimming in warm waters and enjoying her silly trophy husband."

"But she doesn't see it that way?"

"She has a stipulation that she is insistent on before she retires, the details of which have not been worked out yet." Ethan reached for his beer. "So, tell me, Miss Holly Motta, you have come to New York completely on your own?"

What did his aunt want? Was there a family secret?

Holly was dying to know. In fact she wanted to know about all of Ethan's joys and triumphs and struggles and defeats. Wanted to tell him all of hers. Though she couldn't fathom why.

Even if she had been open to meeting the right man—a man with whom she would share the deepest, darkest nooks and crannies of her life—it wouldn't be a man who showered on airplanes.

A man like Ethan Benton had no business with a girl who had grown up in a trailer park in Fort Pierce. *Never going to happen*. And she wasn't looking for someone, anyway. This was *her* time.

She chewed her pizza, suddenly agitated by the way Ethan continued to examine her, as if she was an object he was considering purchasing.

"I have to say I cannot remember the last time I was with a woman who ate half a pizza in one sitting."

"Of course not. You probably only keep company with women who eat one green bean and then tell you how full they are."

That crooked grin broke into a hearty belly laugh. "You are absolutely right. If they eat anything at all. You are definitely not like the women I tend to meet."

"Should I consider that a compliment?"

"Please tell me why you have come to New York alone."

"Who would I have come with if not alone? I haven't seen my mother in years. My brother, Vince, is doing well in Miami. I have no other ties."

She'd grown up strategizing and compensating for her unreliable mother. Looking out for Vince. Then working around Ricky's bad behavior. Juggling two or three jobs. Keeping the house clean. Making sure people were fed. Paying bills. Always being the responsible one. Day after day. Year after year.

"I'm through with being cautious." She couldn't believe she was blathering this out to a man she'd only just met. "Yes, I came to New York alone. No job. No permanent place to live. I don't even know if here's where I belong. That's why I was going to stay in this apartment for a while—to figure it out. I'm sure it all sounds insane to you."

"How it sounds is brave."

Ethan furrowed his brow. A minute ago Holly had confided that she wasn't in contact with her mother. No mention of a father. He sensed there was plenty more that she hadn't said. That she'd been through more than her share of trouble and strife. Although it might be a made-up story meant to evoke sympathy from him to let her stay in the apartment.

Every previous experience he'd had with women other than Aunt Louise had led him to believe that they were never what they seemed.

Starting with his own mother.

Do not trust *trust*. It was a lesson he'd learned decades ago.

That was why he'd devised this scheme to set up a fake relationship, so that Aunt Louise would think she had gotten her wish. She would retire with her mind at ease and her attention on her health.

An imitation fiancée would suit him perfectly. The women he'd known before had always wanted something from him. With this arrangement he'd dreamt up everyone would get what they were after. Clean and upfront, with clear expectations and no disappointment.

After he and Holly had finished eating she retrieved a pad and pencils from her luggage and sat herself in the window, with its second-floor view out onto the street. She turned sideways, somehow wedging her long legs into the windowsill, and propped her sketchpad on her knees.

"You are welcome to pull a chair over," Ethan tossed out, not in the habit of contorting himself to fit into small spaces.

"I'm fine, thanks."

Unsure what to do with himself, he picked up his tablet to check emails. If he'd been there alone, as planned, he would have gone to bed. It was going to be a busy week.

He could ask Holly to take her things into the bedroom. Then he could turn off the lights, try to get comfortable on the sofa and hope to fall asleep.

Yet it was so unusual for him to be in an apartment with someone he craved her company and wanted to prolong it. He wasn't ready for her to retreat to separate quarters.

How crazy was the idea that kept popping into his mind?

As Holly drew, he began telling her more about Aunt

Louise. About the cruel medical condition that was taking away pieces of her.

"How did your family's company get started?" she asked, while working on her drawing.

"With nothing. When my father and Uncle Mel were in their twenties they saved their money from doing carpentry work until they had enough to buy the South Boston apartment they grew up in. Then they bought the whole building. And then the one next to it."

"That takes focus and determination. Hmm…" She shook her head.

"Hmm—what?"

She kept her eyes on her pad. "It's just that nobody I've ever known has done anything like that."

"After my uncle married Louise, she helped them grow the business. My father died twenty-five years ago. Then Aunt Louise took over as CEO when Uncle Mel died five years ago."

Ethan had only vague memories of his father. But he so missed the uncle who had become a second father to him. Melvin Benton had been a smart leader. A just and fair man.

"Uncle Mel would have agreed that it is time for Aunt Louise to step down. Before industry gossip sullies her reputation as the competent successor to his legacy that she was."

"What is it that your aunt wants you to do before she'll agree to retire?"

Oh, so Holly had been paying close attention earlier, when he'd started to tell her about Aunt Louise's request and then stopped himself.

"She wants to see me established in my personal life. For me to have what she and Uncle Mel had. She is waiting for me to be engaged to be married."

"And now you are?"

"So to speak…"

"There's no 'so to speak.' You're either engaged or you're not."

"Not necessarily."

Why had he started this? He'd revealed more than he should have.

"Tell me," she persisted, without looking up.

"I would rather talk about you. You have come to New York with no work here at all? This city can be a very tough place."

"I know. But I do have some people to contact. You're probably thinking my coming to New York was a really reckless bet. But if I didn't do it now I never would have."

When Ethan glanced down to the inbox on his tablet his eyes opened wide at the latest email. It was the talent agency, apologizing for contacting him so late in the evening and asking for the duration of his booking for Penelope Perkins, his soon-to-be "fiancée." Because, the representative explained, Mrs. Perkins had just informed them of her pregnancy. She expected to be available for a few months but, after that her altered appearance might be an issue for any long-term acting assignment.

Good heavens. *Yes*, Mrs. Perkins's blossoming pregnancy was going to be an issue! That would be too much to disguise from Aunt Louise. First an engagement and then a pregnancy right away? Not to mention the fact that Penelope was apparently *Mrs.* Perkins. And a certain *Mr.* Perkins was be unlikely to be agreeable to such an arrangement.

The veins in Ethan's neck pulsed with frustration. As if he didn't have enough to do! Now the engagement plan he'd worked so hard to devise was in jeopardy. Could he choose someone else and get an appointment with her in time? He quickly tabbed through the photos of the other actresses on the website. They were all of a suitable age. Any one of them might do.

Then he glanced up to lovely Holly, sketching in the windowsill.

What if…?

He'd been exchanging pleasant conversation with Holly all evening. Why *not* her? It might work out quite nicely. Perhaps they could have an easy, friendly business partnership based on mutual need. He had a lot he could offer her.

Of course the fact that he found her so interesting was probably *not* a plus. It might add complication. But who was to say that he wouldn't have been attracted to Penelope Perkins, or some other actress he'd chosen?

A sense of chemistry would be palpable to Aunt Louise and anyone else they would encounter. It would make them believable as a couple. And he certainly wouldn't be acting on any impulses. It wasn't as if he was open to a genuine relationship.

A fake fiancée was all he was looking for. Holly was as good a bet as any.

He gazed at her unnoticed for a moment. She turned to a new page on her sketchpad. Then, when she asked him again about whether or not he was engaged, he finally told her the truth.

He picked up the beer he had been drinking with the pizza. Carefully peeling off the label that circled the neck of the bottle, he rolled it into a ring. And then stepped over to Holly in front of the window. Where anyone in New York could be walking by and might look up to see them.

"I was intending to hire an actress," he explained. "But I think Aunt Louise would like you. You remind me of her. There is something very…real about you."

He got down on one knee. Held up the beer label ring in the palm of his hand.

She gasped.

"Holly, I do not suppose you would… If you might con-sider… Would you, please? Can you pretend to marry me?"

CHAPTER THREE

"HEAR ME OUT," Ethan said, still on one knee.

Holly had been so stunned by his proposal that moments stood still in time. It was as if she watched the scene from outside her body.

In an Upper East Side apartment in New York an elegant man with wavy brown hair waited on bended knee after proposing to his dark-haired intended. Would she say yes?

Holly couldn't remember if she had dreamt of a moment like this when she was a little girl. A dashing prince, the romantic gesture of kneeling, white horse at the ready. She'd probably had those fantasies at some point but she couldn't recall them. They were buried under everything else.

Most of Holly's memories were of hard times.

Growing up, it had been her alarm clock that had snapped her out of any dreams she might have had. The clock had made her spring her up quickly to check if her mother had woken up and was getting dressed for work. Or if she wasn't going to get out of bed. Or hadn't made it home at all during the night. Leaving Holly to scrounge together breakfast and a sack lunch for her and Vince.

No, Holly hadn't had much time for fairy-tale dreams. She'd been proposed to before. After all, she'd been married. But Ricky's offer had been about as heartfelt as their marriage had been. It had been on a sweaty, humid day in his beat-up old truck and it had gone something like, "I guess you want to get married..."

At the time, she'd thought that was about as good as it was going to get.

"It would be strictly business, of course." Ethan continued with his proposition. "An engagement in name only."

So Holly's second marriage proposal was to be just as unromantic as her first.

A twinge of despair pinged through her.

Ethan was suggesting a fake engagement to appease his aunt and get her to retire before poor health tarnished her standing. She understood why he was asking, but she didn't see what would be in it for her.

He anticipated her immediate trepidation and added, "We can negotiate a contract that is mutually beneficial."

"That certainly sounds cut and dried, Mr. Benton."

Even having this discussion was making her uncomfortable. Because it brought up notions like a little girl's dreams and happily-ever-afters. Thoughts she couldn't afford to linger on. Not then and not now.

She squinted at him. "Could you please get up?"

"I can."

He rose, yet still held out the beer bottle label. Looking down at it he assured her, "We would purchase a proper engagement ring."

"Let's put the paper ring down for a minute, okay?"

He laid it gently onto the coffee table as if it was a thing of great value. "I have a scenario..." He gestured toward the sofa.

She followed him, but this time didn't sit next to him as she had when they were eating pizza. She chose one of the black chairs opposite him. Best to keep her distance.

"May I be frank?"

"Oh...okay," Holly answered with apprehension.

"You are new to New York. You mentioned that you do

not yet have work. You mentioned that you could not afford to stay in a hotel. I am offering you very easy temporary employment. Pose as my fiancée. What I would pay you will help you establish yourself here. Shall we bring it to the bargaining table? Name your price."

"Name my *price*!" Such a ruthless businessman! Everything was a deal to him. "Are you used to getting everything you want simply by demanding it?"

"Oh, I always get what I want." His stare drilled into her.

Wow, what a predator. And why did that excite her rather than repel her?

Just for entertainment's sake, she took a minute to fantasize what being his pretend fiancée might be like. She'd probably be physically near him quite a bit. He'd have his arm around her shoulder. Sometimes around her waist. They'd hold hands. He'd probably even place a kiss on her cheek in front of other people, just to put on a convincing show.

Holly snuck a glance at his mouth. Ripe lips that looked to be endlessly kissable. No way would a plan that involved her standing close to his lips ever, *ever* be a good idea.

But it didn't matter, because she was just playing along hypothetically. "I'm not for hire by the hour!" She feigned indignation.

"There need not be anything sordid about it, Miss Motta." Ethan eyed the paper ring on the table. "I assure you I am only proposing a trade agreement."

She didn't doubt that. This was a man who'd already said he kept company with stunning, glamorous women who ate one green bean. He'd never be interested in her romantically. She'd have nothing to worry about there.

But she couldn't resist throwing in for fun, "My brother, Vince, is up for a promotion in your Miami office. Let's say this deal included helping him along in his career…"

"Done," Ethan answered quickly. "I would have to look at his human resources file and speak with the people who work with him. But if he is deserving, I would certainly look to promote my future brother-in-law."

He leaned forward. Even though there was the coffee table between them, she could feel him zeroing in on her. Coming in for the kill. Determined to make the sale.

"What else, Miss Motta?"

He was so maddeningly sure of himself. Holly hadn't met many people who were like that.

She sat dumbfounded, way out of her league.

Ethan raised a finger in the air with a thought. "Shall we consider it another way? You need somewhere to live. How about if I give you this apartment? I will put it in your name."

Holly tried to keep her eyes from bugging out. *How about if I give you this apartment?* Who even *said* that?

"As you can imagine, real estate is something I have as a bartering tool. Regardless of what happens, you will have a home in New York."

A home in New York. He really did know how to persuade a deal.

"What is it that might happen?" She had no intention of taking him up on his offer, but she was curious. "How is it that you see this working?"

He'd obviously thought this through well. Today was Monday. His aunt Louise and her boy-toy husband, Fernando, would be coming down from Boston this week in preparation for their Saturday shareholders' gala. He'd present Holly to them on Wednesday night.

"Dinner. Le Cirque. Or one of the new Asian-Spanish fusion restaurants in Tribeca. Something flashy that shows us as a hip New York couple on top of the trends."

"How about instead I throw a pot roast in the slow cooker?" Holly countered, batting him the idea.

His mouth tipped. "A home-cooked meal? Like she and Uncle Mel used to make on Sundays? Brilliant!"

Holly was no gourmet cook, but she knew how to work with the basics. She'd had to learn if she and her brother were ever going to eat. When they were kids she'd search through the pockets of pants left on the floor. Between the couch cushions. Under the seats in the car. Somehow she'd find enough money to buy a few groceries and put a meal together for her and Vince. Restaurant visits had been few and far between.

"Mashed potatoes. Roasted carrots. Apple pie..." She completed the menu.

"Perfect. I will try to be of assistance."

"Continue," she requested.

It was amusing to hear Ethan's outline for the masquerade that she wasn't actually going to be any part of.

Their next appearance would be at the shareholders' gala on Saturday, where Holly would be formally introduced as Ethan's fiancée.

"So I'd look amazing that night? Dress? Jewels? Hair and makeup? The whole nine yards?"

He sat silent for a minute, as if lost in his own memories. But then he snapped back with, "Of course. A couture gown would be chosen for you. My tuxedo tie will match your attire."

"It'd be a crime if it didn't."

Then there would be an engagement party in Boston. A month or so later would come the announcement that Aunt Louise was stepping down. A grand retirement luncheon would send her off in style.

"In between those dates," Ethan explained, "I would travel, so that you and I should not have to attend many events together. I will devise reasons that I have to spend prolonged periods in Florence or Sydney or the like."

Ethan went on. After those appearances Aunt Louise

and Fernando would move to Barbados as planned. Ethan and Holly—the happy couple—would fly to the island for long weekends three or four times during the first year. In between those visits Holly would be free to live the life she chose, as long as there was nothing criminal or anything that attracted attention.

Then they'd evaluate. They could continue to visit Aunt Louise and make excuses as to why they hadn't yet married. Or they could tell fibs about a lavish wedding that would take an entire year to plan.

"Or," he continued, "especially if you were to meet someone else and need to be free, we could call off the engagement. Aunt Louise would be settled into her island life of leisure. By that point there would not be any danger of her wanting to return to frigid Boston and the working grind."

"And what if *you* were the one to meet someone?" she clipped, pretending to advocate a deal for herself.

"Impossible!" he spat immediately. "I will never marry."

His harshness hit her like a slap in the face.

Or perhaps it was a warning.

"I see," she assured him, and knew she'd understood his underlying message.

"Therefore, when we split up, you will own this apartment outright—which you can either keep, lease or sell. And the engagement ring. And whatever clothing and jewels have been purchased. Your brother's position will be secure. We can also agree on a monetary settlement. In exchange for very little labor on your part, I can provide you with a lifetime of comfort and luxury."

Game over.

Enough was enough.

Even if it could be as simple as he made it sound she had come to New York to get her own life straightened out. Not to get tangled up in someone else's.

"Ethan, I appreciate the offer. And I think it's great that you've done so much planning on this. It shows how much you care about your aunt. But this is not for me."

He swallowed hard. His Adam's apple bobbed in his throat. His jaw tightened.

Was he upset?

Of course. This was a man who was used to getting everything he wanted. It wasn't personal. She was a mere obstacle for him to overcome in order to reach his goal.

Ethan tapped his tablet. "Holly Motta dot com—is that it?"

She nodded, yes. What was he up to?

He typed.

"Huh…" His thumb slid through what she assumed to be her website's gallery. "Huh…"

What was he thinking? She took great pride in her work. Suddenly it mattered to her what he thought of it. Which was silly, because his opinion was of no concern to her at all. Yet she sat on the edge of the chair, spine held stiff as she waited for a comment.

His thumb continued to swipe the tablet.

"Hmm…" His next sound was at a higher pitch than the one before. It sounded like approval.

"Why are you looking at my website?"

Ethan ignored the question and continued. His finger slid less frequently. He was spending more time on each piece of work.

Holly imagined what it might feel like to have that thumb slide across her cheek instead of the tablet screen. Or slowly down the center of her chest. That thumb and its nine partners on those two big hands looked as if they'd always know exactly what to do.

More fantasy. She hadn't been touched in a long, long time.

Finally Ethan looked from the screen to her. "These are extraordinary."

"Thank you," she breathed with gratification—and relief.

He raised a finger in the air again. "Perhaps we can negotiate a merger that would be satisfying to both of us."

She squished her eyebrows.

"In exchange for you posing as my fiancée, as I have outlined, you will be financially compensated and you will become legal owner of this apartment and any items such as clothes and jewels that have been purchased for this position. Your brother's career will not be impacted negatively should our work together come to an end. *And...*" He paused for emphasis.

Holly leaned forward in her chair, her back still board-straight.

"I have a five-building development under construction in Chelsea. There will be furnished apartments, office lofts and common space lobbies—all in need of artwork. I will commission you for the project."

Holly's lungs emptied. A commission for a big corporate project. That was exactly what she'd hoped she'd find in New York. A chance to have her work seen by thousands of people. The kind of exposure that could lead from one job to the next and to a sustained and successful career.

This was all too much. Fantastic, frightening, impossible... Obviously getting involved in any way with Ethan Benton was a terrible idea. She'd be beholden to him. Serving another person's agenda again. Just what she'd come to New York to get away from.

But this could be a once-in-a-lifetime opportunity. An apartment. A job. It sounded as if he was open to most any demand she could come up with. She really did owe it to herself to contemplate this opportunity.

Her brain was no longer operating normally. The clock on Ethan's desk reminded her that it was after midnight. She'd left Fort Pierce early that morning.

"That really is an incredible offer…" She exhaled. "But I'm too tired to think straight. I'm going to need to sleep on it."

"As you wish."

Holly moved to collect the luggage she'd arrived with. Ethan beat her to it and hoisted the duffel bag over his shoulder. He wrenched the handle of the suitcase. Its wheels tottered as fast as her mind whirled as she followed him to the bedroom.

"Good night, then." He placed the bags just inside the doorway and couldn't get out of the room fast enough.

Before closing the door she poked her head out and called, "Ethan Benton, you don't play fair."

Over his shoulder, he turned his face back toward her. "I told you. I always get what I want."

Holly shut the door with her bare foot and leaned back against it. She pursed her lips together to keep from screaming. Her heart thumped so loud she was sure Ethan would hear it in the other room. *Goodness gracious.*

Ethan Benton and his proposition were quite simply the most exciting things that had ever happened to her!

A rush went through her as she recalled that devilish grin creeping slowly up his mouth. Those deep brown eyes that had stayed glued on her, assuring her he was listening to her when she spoke.

Holly hadn't talked and listened as much as she had tonight in a long time. She hadn't dated anyone since leaving Ricky the Rat two years ago. With her in Fort Pierce and Vince a two-hour drive away in Miami, she usually saw her brother twice a month. There was a girls' night here and there with friends. That was about it.

She hadn't really thought about it, but now when she did she realized she led a fairly solitary existence. Hopefully New York would jostle that, along with everything else.

But the change *wasn't* going to come by stepping into Ethan Benton's life. Although it might be the most fun she'd ever have. A jet-set world she'd only read about in magazines… Who wouldn't want to dash off to Barbados for long weekends? To walk on pink sand with her toes in sparkling blue water. Attend glitzy parties…throw some of her own. Buy clothes without looking at the price tag. Never worry about where the rent or her next meal was coming from. Have the best of everything.

It would be amazing—even if it was only for a short time—to be completely taken care of. After all those years of putting other people ahead of her.

Which reminded her of how this deal could benefit her brother. Becoming part of the Benton family, even in name only, might help him further his career in a way he'd never have the chance to otherwise. He'd get to spend more time with Ethan and Louise. They'd see up close how capable and special he was.

No. This wasn't about Vince. He'd be fine on his own. He was a grown man and his career was underway.

It was time for *her* future to begin. Period. In the morning she would tell Ethan no.

Besides, once he heard that she had already been married and divorced he wouldn't think she was an appropriate choice for his game.

Right now, she needed to get some sleep.

She stopped short at the sight of the room's king-size bed. This was where Ethan Benton had been planning to lay that tall, sturdy frame of his tonight. A wiggle shot up her spine at the mental image of him stretched out on this bed. Perhaps only wearing the plaid pajama bottoms as when she'd first seen him on the sofa.

On the bed she counted one, two…eight plush pillows, overlapped in a tidy row against the brown leather headboard. She imagined Ethan's head against those pillows, with that curl of hair tousled on his forehead.

The luxury pillowcases alternated in color, tan then black. Which coordinated with the tightly fitted tan sheets. She ran a finger along the black duvet, tracing it down the right side of the bed. Then across the bottom. Then up the left. It was all too matchy-matchy for her tastes, but clearly made of expensive fabrics.

She eyed the wall-to-wall closet. If she took Ethan up on his proposal it would become filled with designer gowns for glamorous black tie dinners. Trendy separates for groundbreaking ceremonies. Classic sportswear for sailing jaunts and tennis tournaments. The finest shoes and purses and jewels.

None of that was her. She couldn't picture it. Not even for make-believe.

Back on earth, Holly didn't know whether she should unpack her suitcase full of jeans, comfortable skirts and tee shirts. She slid the blond wood closet door open to see if anything was inside.

Four men's suits hung neatly on wooden hangers, with breathing room in between each. Dark gray, light gray, navy pinstripe and a beautiful maroon. They looked to be Ethan's size. He'd probably look especially handsome in that maroon. It would go well with his brown eyes and that brown hair with its speckles of red.

There were freshly laundered shirts. Complementary ties. Polished shoes. A tuxedo and its accessories. Two pairs of pressed jeans. A pair of casual boots. She resisted the temptation to open any drawers. She had seen an overcoat and a leather jacket on the coat rack by the front door.

It wasn't a large wardrobe. Ethan had said he traveled a lot, but hadn't mentioned how long he was staying in New York.

She fingered the lapel of the maroon suit jacket. Ricky

the Rat had only owned one wrinkly black suit. She could count on one hand the times he'd worn it. He was the jeans and workboots type. There were times she'd thought he was sexy.

One of the times he hadn't been sexy was when she'd come home from work early one day and the workboots were all he'd had on. While he was in bed with their neighbor Kiki.

The rain was heavier outside now. Holly watched the bedroom window being pounded with sheets of the downpour. A rumble of thunder emphasized the storm's strength. *Good.* Let it wash away her past.

Deciding to leave her suitcase on the floor for the night, she pulled back the duvet on the bed and climbed into the king-size reminder of the man who was already making her feel as if she were spiraling away from her old life. Even though her encounter with him would come to an end in the morning, her transition to something new had begun.

The bed was divine. The mattress firm. The sheets crisp. She pulled the thick cover over her. Beyond comfortable, she nestled in the oasis, away from cares and plans. It was a peaceful heaven on earth after such a long day. Time to rest her body and mind. She was going to sleep like a log...

Two hours later Holly tossed and turned with exasperation. She hadn't kept her eyes shut for more than a minute before her brain had assaulted her with more and more opinions.

What Ethan was proposing could be her lucky break. A commission to do the artwork for his big development in Chelsea... A chance to really get started in New York...

She'd come to the city armed with work references, but the life of an artist could be tricky. Maybe nothing would pan out from the names and phone numbers she'd collected. Or she'd get small jobs here and there but they might not lead to anything else.

Ethan's proposition was a multi-phase project that would probably be six months of work at least. In that time she could really put down roots here.

She was determined to make her entire living as an artist. Not to have to work anymore as a maid or a nanny during the lean times. Her goals were clear. New York was the place where dreams were made or broken. If it didn't work out here, so be it—but she was certainly going to take her shot.

Imagine how much easier it would be without any astronomical rent to pay. New York apartment prices were notoriously high. Holly knew that she would probably have to live with a roommate. Maybe several of them. Some might have come to New York for the twenty-four-hour-a-day lifestyle, for the party that never ended. The household might be full of noise and people and activity at all hours of the day and night. It might prevent Holly from getting her work done or resting when she needed to.

Or she might end up with people who were slobs. Not able to tolerate a dirty mess, she would end up cleaning up after them. Cleaning up after people—how much of her life had she already spent doing that? She'd never minded taking care of her brother, but her ex-husband hadn't ever seemed even to know where the trash can or the washing machine were. Nor had her mother.

Maybe these roommate slobs wouldn't pay their share of their rent and she'd get evicted. She might end up having to move from place to place through no fault of her own. That would be maddening.

Ethan was offering work and a place to live. This tasteful apartment all to herself. It was one thing to be allowed to stay here while she looked for a place. It was quite another to have it *belong* to her. She could paint here. Reposition the furniture in the living room to make the most of the natural light.

Wait a minute.

Part of Ethan's bargain was that he would pay her. She would be able to afford to rent studio space. A New York artist with her own studio... If *that* wasn't a dream come true!

But on the other hand...

And she needed to consider...

She couldn't really...

And then what...?

When Holly opened her eyes, a drizzly morning sky crept in through the window. At some point she had finally dozed off, her mind twirling about the past and what the future could hold. Now, with morning's dawn in Ethan Benton's bedroom, certainty hit her like a ton of bricks.

If something seemed too good to be true, it was.

Not cut out to be anyone's pretend anything, Holly was only who she was. Ethan was kidding himself. It could only end in disaster. She would do him a favor by acknowledging the impossibility of his proposal, even though he wasn't able to see it for himself.

His judgment was clouded by his deep love for his aunt Louise. How touching was his concern for her welfare, for her reputation and her happiness. Blood ran thick. A good man took his family responsibilities seriously...

She had to call her brother. She wouldn't tell him about Ethan's offer. But she *did* need his help sorting out this confusion about her staying in the apartment. It would be good to hear his voice. In the end, he was the only one she really had in her corner.

He'd be working out in the garage of the little house he rented in Miami. Lifting weights. Bench pressing and hoisting dumbbells before showering and getting to work at Benton.

"Vinz." She pictured him, no doubt in a muscle shirt drenched in sweat. His close-cropped blond hair so unlike her black. The round blue eyes marking him as her kin.

"Holz! How's the Big Apple so far?"

She explained the mix-up with the apartment.

Vince promised to make some calls as soon as he got into the office. "I'll get it fixed," he assured her.

"I don't know if you can."

"Listen to me, big sis. We're going to sniff out opportunities for you and you're going take them. You'll grab everything that's thrown your way."

"Yeah."

"Remember—straight up or fall down!" He chanted their lifelong rally call—the desperate bravado of two kids with no one but each other to root for them.

After hanging up, Holly held the phone in her hand and stared absently out the window for a while. Thick clouds in the sky moved horizontally across her vision.

There had always been rainy days. No one knew how many more were ahead. It would be such a gift to have an umbrella.

Finally she tossed the phone onto the bed and opened the door.

Ethan was in the kitchen. She watched him start a pot of coffee before he noticed she was there. When he did, she leaned against the doorway. Her hair was probably a mess. Surely she had bags under her eyes from her fitful night. She lifted her hand and looked at her fingers with their perpetual paint around the cuticles and under the nails. She was who she was.

"Okay, Ethan. I'll marry you."

CHAPTER FOUR

SHE SAID YES! Ethan wanted to shout it from the rooftops. *She said yes!*

His blood coursed. His muscles tingled.

She said yes!

And then he caught himself. *Good heavens.* There was no cause for fireworks to be launched from his heart. There was no reason to announce his undying devotion in front of the citizens of Manhattan. He was not a giddy groom filled with bliss and anticipation.

A woman he'd met yesterday had agreed to a jointly beneficial contract. He signed deals every day. This was just another one.

With a flick on the switch of the coffeepot he shook his head, trying to dislodge the obvious cobwebs in his skull.

He'd gotten a bit carried away.

Truthfully, he hadn't been alone with a woman in a long time—and certainly not in the close quarters of a small apartment. Perhaps that had stirred up a primal reaction in him. While the mating ritual wasn't part of his daily life, it *was* a natural phenomenon.

Although Ethan employed thousands of women in all aspects of his business, he shunned intimate social situations with them as much as possible. Keeping a clear and level head was what he did best. Women were distracting. Distractions were to be avoided. Problem—solution.

This was the first lesson he needed in order to carry off his plan. He was going to be spending a lot of time with an attractive woman. He'd need to guard and defend himself against her feminine charms. It wasn't personal. It didn't matter whether it was Holly, pregnant Penelope Perkins or another actress he'd picked from a photograph.

In three measured breaths, with his face toward the coffeepot, he set his focus. *Guard and defend.*

Then he turned to Holly, still standing in the doorway. Dark cascades of hair fell around her pretty face, which had a just-woken flush in her cheeks. Her tee shirt was definitely not concealing a bra.

Involuntarily, his body began to lean toward hers. A kiss pushed forward from his lips.

Guard and defend!

In the nick of time, he pulled himself back. Her allure was something he'd need to get accustomed to. His body's involuntary response to her worried him...told him that might be difficult.

But he would be triumphant. For the sake of Aunt Louise he could conquer anything.

Ethan directed himself to talk, since he couldn't kiss. "How did you sleep?"

"Great," she lied.

Her eyes looked tired. He hadn't got much sleep, either. He was far too tall to stretch out comfortably on that sofa. Plus, his mind had taunted him with replays of the evening.

"That coffee smells good," she said as she massaged the back of her neck.

"It does. How do you take it?"

"Lots of milk or cream. No sugar."

Ethan opened one of the cabinets to look for cups. It held only drinking glasses. He hadn't spent enough time in this apartment to know where everything was kept. His second try yielded large white mugs. Setting them on the black granite countertop, he poured the steaming coffee.

The kitchen was Manhattan Minimal. Pint-size efficiency. Cabinets, sink and dishwasher on one side. Stove and refrigerator on the other. A one-person kitchen. Too cramped for two people to work in.

Which was why when Holly stepped in to open the fridge he felt her hips brush past him. In turn, his hips reacted of their own volition—which, fortunately, she didn't notice.

"What are we eating for breakfast?' she asked as she peered into the refrigerator.

"What do we have?" He'd only had bottles of water when he'd got in yesterday, and beer last night with the pizza.

"Eggs, butter and cheese. And the bread and fruit." She pointed to the baskets on the counter. "We can work with this."

The way she said *we* made Ethan's ears prick up. He wasn't used to *we*. He'd worked very hard at avoiding *we*. This was no time to start. Although for the first time he was curious about *we*. He reasoned that this fake engagement was a perfect way of safely pretending to experience *we*, with both parties knowing fully well that the truth was *me* and *me* achieving individual goals.

Right. However, now it felt somewhat confusing.

Holly pulled the carton of milk out of the fridge and handed it to him. Ethan was keenly aware of their fingertips touching during the exchange.

She laid ingredients on the counter. "How does cheese omelets, toasted bagels and sliced fruit sound?"

"What do you generally eat for breakfast?"

Holly giggled. A bit of blush rose in her cheeks. *How adorable*. "Was that a get-to-know-each-other question?"

"It was. If we are going to be convincing as an engaged couple, we have to know those sorts of things about each other."

He handed her a mug. She took a slow sip and exhaled her satisfaction.

"You put the perfect amount of milk in my cup, so we must be off to a good start."

Ethan felt ridiculously proud that she liked her coffee.

"How do you take yours?" she went up.

"Also without sugar. But not as much milk."

"I'll eat anything…" She went back to his question. "If we hadn't polished off that pizza, that's great cold in the morning."

"Cold pizza? Noted."

"Do you know how to cook?"

"I could probably manage to broil a steak without ruining it."

"Eggs?"

"Not really," he confessed.

"Today you learn, then."

"Is that so?"

"I'll put on a show for your aunt Louise, but surely you don't think I'm going to be cooking and cleaning for you." Her face stilled in a moment of earnest uncertainty. "*Do* you?"

"Of course not, phony fiancée."

"It's just that I've done plenty of taking care of people in my life. I just want to take care of myself."

Holly had been through a lot. He'd been able to tell that about her from the start—had seen it right through her spunky attitude. She was no fresh-faced hopeful, arriving in New York full of delusions and fantasies. There was a past. A past that he suspected included hardship and pain.

Another one of those innate urges told him to wrap his arms around her and promise that he'd make up for all her hurts. That now she would be the one taken care of. That he'd quite like to make it his life's mission to take care of her in every possible way.

Once again he had to chastise himself sternly. He had merely hired her to perform a service. For which she would be paid very well. With that opportunity she would be able to find whatever she'd come to New York to get. She didn't need him.

The agony of that shocked him. A reminder to guard and defend.

Holly handed him the carton of eggs. She gave him a bowl. "Four."

Finding a cutting board and a knife, Holly sliced cheese while Ethan cracked eggs. They stood side by side at their tasks, each dependent on the other in order to get the job done. Ethan appreciated teamwork. That was what made Benton Worldwide, and every other successful venture work. It must be the same in a marriage.

Two bagels were halved and popped into the toaster.

"Frying pan?" she mused to herself, and quickly moved to his other side to find one.

His mind flipped back to the past. To Aunt Louise and Uncle Melvin. It had been almost ten years since they'd done the normal things that married couples did. Mel had died over five years ago. Before that recurrences of his cancer had often had him bedridden. But they'd had moments like these. Hundreds, even thousands of cozy day-to-day moments like preparing breakfast.

Those moments strung together added up to a life shared between two people.

In reality, with their success and privilege it was not as if Aunt Louise and Uncle Mel had often been in the kitchen frying up eggs. But they had always cooked Sunday supper together whenever they could. It had been one of their signatures.

Ethan had potent memories of the two of them together as a couple. The way they'd been with each other. Even if it they had just been at the front door on the way out, helping each other layer on coats, scarves and hats to brave the Boston winter. How they'd maneuvered around each other. With effortless choreography. Totally at ease with each other, aware of each other's moves, each other's needs, each other's comforts.

He understood why Aunt Louise so wanted that same security for him. Why she was concerned with the way he jetted around the globe, working all the time, never stopping, never settling. The wisdom of age had shown her what might happen to a man who didn't balance power and labor with the other things that made life worth living. Family. Love.

But his aunt should accept that after all Ethan had been through love wasn't an option for him. He would never open his heart. Her destiny wasn't his. Yet he couldn't blame her for wishing things were different. That his past hadn't defined his future.

In reflection, Aunt Louise had valued her relationship with Uncle Mel above everything else in her life. She'd had a love so true it had never let her down.

Unlike him.

This ruse was the best solution. If the knowledge that Ethan was engaged to be married made Aunt Louise happy, and put her mind at ease, then he'd have taken good care of her. Ethan was in charge of all decisions now, and he wanted them to be in his aunt's best interests.

He and Holly sat down at the table with their breakfast. Just as she had with the pizza last night, she dug in like a hungry animal. She took big bites and didn't try to disguise her obvious pleasure.

Ethan asked if maybe she had gone hungry as a child.

"My mother was…unpredictable."

Something he himself knew more than a little about. Anger burned his throat.

A bittersweet smile crossed her mouth as she cut circular slices of an orange and handed one to him. "Vince and I used to call these rings of sunshine. There were always oranges in Florida."

He wanted to know how she'd been wronged. But he wasn't going to walk on that common ground.

"Aunt Louise and Fernando are coming for dinner on Wednesday." He cut to the matter at hand. "We need to prepare. Our first order of business is making this apartment look like we truly live here. We will start with…"

"The artwork!" they chimed in unison.

"We will visit my favorite galleries in Soho. You can make the final selection."

Outside, stormy skies had given way to more hard rain. "Dress accordingly."

He plucked his phone from his pocket and began tapping.

Half an hour later, a stocky man in a suit and chauffeur's cap held a car door open for Holly.

"This is my driver, Leonard," Ethan introduced.

"Ma'am."

Holly darted into the black car without getting too wet from the downpour. Sliding across the tan leather backseat, she made room for Ethan beside her. Leonard shut the passenger door and hurried around to the driver's seat.

As they pulled away from the apartment building, Ethan activated the privacy glass that separated the front seat from the back.

Holly didn't know what she'd gotten herself into. Fear and excitement rattled her at the same time.

Soho galleries and shareholders' galas… She didn't really know how she was going to fake her way through a life so different from hers. Being ferried around New York in a town car with a privacy glass.

Ethan had clearly noticed her discomfort at his shielding his driver from any conversation they were going to have. "Obviously we need complete discretion to pull off our little enterprise, do we not?"

"Yup."

"Off we go, then. Yes?"

As crazy as it was, she'd already said yes to this wild ride with him. "Yes."

She watched New York though the car window. The city was gorgeous in the rain. Buildings seemed even taller and grander beneath the turbulent skies. People in dark clothes with umbrellas hurried along the sidewalks. To her eyes, they looked as if they were from a bygone era. Her mind snapped mental pictures. She wanted to paint all of it.

While Ethan checked messages on his phone Holly was aware of every breath he took. Her lungs couldn't help synchronizing each of his inhales and exhales with her own. They were so near each other on the seat her leg rested along his. She detected a faint smell of his woodsy shampoo.

You'll get used to him, she told herself. *Soon enough, he won't be so enchanting.*

Ethan touched his phone and brought the device to his ear.

"Nathan. Did you receive my text? Have you made all of the appointments for today?"

He nodded once as he listened.

"Diane—got it. Jeremy—got it. Thank you. Set me up for meetings next week with Con East and the Jersey City contractors."

He looked toward Holly and licked his top lip, although she was sure he didn't realize he had.

"I will be in New York for a while this time. As a matter of fact I have quite the announcement to make at the shareholders' gala."

A squiggle shot up Holly's back. No one had ever looked at her the way he did.

Ethan sent a sincere laugh into the phone. "All right, Nathan. I suppose I can spare you your beheading. *This* time."

He clicked off the call. "That explains the mystery about the apartment. Nathan had me booked in for the same dates but next month. You were right—it was meant to be yours. But now, to everyone concerned, the apartment is *ours.*"

Holly pulled up the collar on her leather jacket as Leonard shuttled them downtown.

Curbside at the first gallery, Leonard helped them out of the car. And then back in as they made their way to the second. And then to the third.

Naturally the staff at each were overjoyed to see Ethan. They reminisced about art openings and museum dedications. Holly felt completely out of place, with nothing to add to the conversations. But she held her own, making intelligent comments about the art on display.

Ethan didn't mention anything about their upcoming nuptials. That announcement was for the gala. Instead he introduced Holly as a friend and painter from Florida whom he had been lucky enough to enlist for an upcoming commission.

Back in the town car again, they munched on the fancy sandwiches Ethan had had Leonard pick up from a gourmet shop. They discussed the paintings they had seen. Holly wanted two, and explained why she'd chosen them.

"If we had more time I'd have my brother send up some canvases that he's storing for me," she said. "If it was really our apartment I'd like to have my own work on the walls."

"I would like that, too," Ethan agreed, with such unexpected warmth it stretched at her heart.

He was masterful at throwing her off-kilter. When

they'd been making breakfast that morning she'd had the feeling several times that he was going to kiss her. At one moment she had desperately hoped he would, while in the next she'd known she must turn away.

Ethan Benton was a bundle of inconsistencies.

Such a precise way he used a paper napkin to brush away imagined crumbs from the corners of his mouth. He was so definite about everything he did. Hobnobbing with gallery people or eating take-out lunch in the car—he did everything with finesse.

It wasn't as if any crumb would dare stick to those glorious lips. Men who showered on planes didn't get food on their faces.

Yet Holly knew there was something damaged underneath all Ethan's confidence and class...

"Can I paint you?"

He contemplated the question as he slowly popped the seal on his bottle of artisan soda.

"You know those drab black and whites of the tree and the flower on the wall?" she went on.

Last night when they'd been critiquing those photographs, flickers had flown between them.

"Flat, corporate..."

"Impersonal," she finished. "That's where I'd hang a painting of you. It would bring personality to the whole room and really make it ours."

"Yes..." he concurred with reluctance. "I suppose it would."

In a flash, Holly understood his hesitation. People were often uncomfortable at the prospect of her painting them. It involved trust. They had to be reassured that she wasn't going to accentuate their pointy nose or, worse still, the loneliness in their eyes.

A good portrait exposed someone's secrets. What was it that Ethan was worried she would reveal to the world?

"Can I?"

"I doubt we could get a painting done in two days' time."

"Let me show you."

Once people had seen Holly's work, she was able to put them at ease. She pulled out her phone and thumbed to her website. "I don't know if you saw these when you were on my site last night. But look. I don't do a typical portrait."

She showed him the screen. "I call them painted sketches. See how they're a bit abstract? And not all that detailed? I would just catch the essence of you."

He whipped his head sideways to face her. "What makes you think you know the essence of me?" he challenged.

Holly's throat jammed at the confrontation. He was right. She *didn't* know him. They'd met yesterday.

But she knew she could get something. Those big and expressive eyes. And, yes, there was some kind of longing behind them.

She might not know him, but she wanted to. This morning at breakfast he had been visibly shaken when she'd hinted at the hardships she'd endured. She had sensed some kind of connection there—a fierce similarity.

She hadn't explicitly told him about the mother who had never consistently provided food for her children. She hadn't mentioned the father who'd come around every couple of years with promises he'd never kept. How Holly had often had to fend for her younger brother and herself.

Yet the damage that dwelled behind Ethan's eyes had made her want to lay her pain bare to him. And for him to lay all his beside hers. As if in that rawness their wounds could be healed.

But none of that was ever to be. They were business partners. Nothing more. Besides, she wasn't going to make herself vulnerable to anyone ever again.

"Never mind." She called his bluff. "I guess we won't

ever find out how much of the real you I could get on a canvas."

One side of his mouth hiked. "I did not say no."

"So you'll let me paint you?"

"I will have you know right now that I have very little patience for sitting still."

"You probably had to sit for family portraits with Aunt Louise and Uncle Mel, right? Dressed up in uncomfortable Christmas clothes by the fireplace? The dutiful family dog by your side? It was torture. You had to sit without moving for what seemed like an eternity."

"I absolutely hated having to hold one position while a greasy bald man who smelled like pipe tobacco painted us."

Flirty words tumbled out of her mouth before she could sensor them. "I promise I'll smell a lot better than the bald man did."

"No doubt."

"And it won't take long."

"I think it might."

Were they still talking about painting?

He lowered the glass separating them from the driver. "Leonard, we are going to change our next stop to Wooster and Broome."

Leonard let them out in front of a painting supplies store the likes of which Holly had never been in before.

She ordered a lot of her materials online, because there were no shops in Fort Pierce that carried fine products like these. When she was low on money she'd make do with what was available at the local brand-name craft store, that also sold knitting yarn and foam balls for school projects.

She cowered at another memory of her ex-husband. As usual, Ricky hadn't wanted to go shopping with her because he thought painting was silly and that she should spend more time going to motorcycle races with him.

Yelling at her to hurry up while she picked out some tubes of paint, Ricky had lost his patience. With a flick of his hand he'd knocked down a display of Valentine's Day supplies. Heart-shaped cardboard boxes, Cupid cutouts and red and pink pompoms had crashed to the floor as Ricky stormed out of the store.

Humiliated, Holly had been left to make apologies and pay for his outburst.

It had been a few months later that she'd caught Ricky in bed with their neighbor. But she'd known that day in the craft store that she couldn't stay married to him.

Now here she was, a million miles away in Soho, the mecca of the American art world, with another man who would never be right for her. Although in completely opposite ways.

Life had a sense of humor.

She chose an easel, stretched canvases in several sizes, new paint and brushes, and palettes and sketchpads, pastels and charcoals. All top-notch. This was the Holly equivalent of a kid in a candy shop.

At the checkout, Ethan opened up an account for her. "That way you can pick up whatever tools and materials you need for Benton projects."

"My goodness…" Her eyes bugged out. "Thank you."

"Of course, my dearest." He winked. "And the next item on the agenda is buying my pretty fiancée some proper clothes."

CHAPTER FIVE

"WHAT'S WRONG WITH my clothes?" Holly demanded as Leonard helped them out of the car in front of a Fifth Avenue shopping mecca.

"Not a thing. You do the artist with paint on her hands bit quite well. All you need is a French cigarette in your mouth and a beret on your head," Ethan answered.

"Very funny."

He laid his hand on the center of her back to guide her through the store's revolving entrance door. Holly's shoulders perked up at his touch.

"However," he continued as they bustled through the busy sales floor, "there is the shareholders' gala, and then there'll be charity dinners and social occasions we will be attending. As we discussed, this arrangement necessitates an appropriate wardrobe."

When they reached the Personal Styling department, an older blonde woman in a sleeveless black dress and pearls was awaiting their arrival.

"Are you Diane?" Ethan extended his right hand. "My assistant, Nathan, spoke with you earlier."

"It's a pleasure to meet you, Mr. Benton." Diane took his outstretched hand with both of hers.

"This is my friend Holly Motta."

"Oh…" Diane gave her a limp handshake, taking notice of the paint under Holly's fingernails.

"Hi!" Holly chirped.

She was going to have to get used to the surprise in people's voices when they met her. Everyone probably knew Ethan as a wealthy playboy who dated fashion models and princesses of small countries. He'd have no reason to be with a mere mortal like her.

Ethan raised his eyebrows at Holly, which made her giggle and feel more at ease.

He peered straight into Holly's eyes while he spoke to the other woman. "Diane, my friend will be accompanying me to numerous events. She is an artist, with little need for formal clothes. Can you help us outfit her in a way that stays true to her creative and unique self?"

Holly's mouth dropped open. Could anyone have said anything more perfect? He wanted to buy her clothes but he didn't want to change her.

Diane was stunned as well. "Cer…certainly," she stuttered. "Can I offer you a glass of champagne?"

And thus began her trip to Fantasyland. While Ethan sipped bubbly on a purple velvet settee, Diane showed Holly into a private dressing room that was larger than all the fitting rooms in the discount shops she usually went to put together.

Six full-length mirrors were positioned to allow for a three-hundred-and-sixty-degree view. The carpet was cream-colored, as was the furniture—no doubt chosen so as not to compete with the clothes. A vanity table with padded chair was ready for any primping needs. Hats, gloves, scarves and purses had been pre-selected and lay waiting in a glass display case. A collection of shoes stood neatly on a shoe rack. Jackets and coats hung from pegs.

Diane ducked away behind one of the mirrors.

Holly whistled out loud as she took it all in. And then

laughed at her predicament. She'd overheard Ethan talking on the phone in the car about a Diane. And a Jeremy. He had prearranged the gallery visits and now this, too. And Holly had thought *herself* to be the taking-care-of-business type! She could take a lesson from him.

"We'll start with daywear," Diane announced as she wheeled in a rack of clothes.

Besides the fact that there hadn't been any money when she was growing up, Holly had never been especially interested in clothes. She dressed functionally and comfortably, and ended up staining most everything with paint anyway. But if she had ever dreamt of wearing stylish garments made of luxurious materials these would be them.

The first ensemble Holly tried on was a white pantsuit. The slim line of the trousers made her legs look eight feet long. And the coordinating blazer with its thin satin lapels was both distinguished and chic. Worn with a navy silk shirt unbuttoned one notch past prim, the outfit delivered "sexy" as well.

Diane moved in quickly to pin the jacket's waist for a trimmer fit.

She suggested Holly try a brown slingback shoe, then plucked the proper size from a stack of boxes waiting at the ready. Diane might be a bit snobby, but she sure as heck knew what she was doing.

"Perhaps you'd like to add a touch of lipstick?" Diane inquired—a polite way of reminding Holly that she'd need to attend to her makeup and hair.

Diane opened a drawer in the vanity table that contained a palette of options. Holly dabbed on some lip gloss, undid her ponytail and brushed her hair. Surveying herself in the mirror, she knew this was without question the best she had ever looked.

"Shall we show Mr. Benton?" Diane suggested.

When Holly stepped into the waiting lounge that

seemed destined for wealthy boyfriends and mothers of brides, Ethan was busy typing into his phone.

He leaned comfortably back on the settee with one leg crossed over the other knee. Effortless elegance. Although the wavy reddish-brown hair that always had a bit of a tousle to it made sure hints of his untamed side came through.

Ethan glanced up. His eyes went through her and then right back down to his phone.

Holly was delighted as recognition gradually took hold. His jaw slackened. Eyebrows bunched. Nostrils flared.

Only then did his eyes rise up again for the double-take.

And take her in he did, indeed. Ever so slowly. From the tip of her head to the pointy toes of her designer shoes. His gaze was wicked. As if she was standing in front of him naked rather than dressed in this finery. The feeling thrilled and aroused her down to her core.

That smile made its way millimeter by millimeter across Ethan's face. "My, my…"

"So you approve?" she flirted.

"To say the least."

"Do you want to see more?"

Focused on the opening of her shirt, where perhaps that questionable button should have been closed but wasn't, he sighed. "I would most *definitely* like to see more."

She pivoted, and when her face was out of view from him let a satisfied grin explode. This was so much fun. She was long overdue for some harmless fun. *Harmless*, right?

Diane helped her into the next outfit and pinned it for alterations. Another silk blouse—this one black, with a square neckline and a gold zipper down the back—tucked into a tan pencil skirt. The look was dressy, but edgy.

Ethan's reaction was all she could have hoped for as he lingered over the snug fit of the skirt across her hips.

Next, dark wash jeans tucked into boots and a flowing

white blouse were complemented by Holly's own black leather jacket.

"More," Ethan demanded.

A crisp red dress with a pleated skirt, short sleeves and matching belt provided a timeless silhouette.

A silver satin cocktail dress draped her curves without being tight. At the sight of her in that one, Ethan shifted in his seat.

As a kid, Holly had sprouted up early and had always been the tallest girl in her class. She remembered feeling big and awkward. It had taken her years to train herself out of slouching her shoulders forward. Slim, but with hips wider than was proportionate to her small bustline, she'd never thought she wore clothes well.

Until today.

With Diane's wizardry to pinch here and fold there, these clothes looked as if they'd been custom-made to flatter her perfectly.

In all, ten outfits were put together, ranging from casual to semi-formal. Extra pieces would be added to mix and match.

Ethan had promised that no matter what happened with their phony engagement the clothes would be hers to keep. That had meant nothing to Holly when he'd said it, but now she understood how important an offer that was.

In these outfits she was *distinctive*. They made a statement. The woman who wore them was someone to take seriously. These were clothes that were the epitome of good taste, that she could—and would—care for and wear for years to come.

But the *pièce de resistance* came when Diane brought out an evening gown for the black-tie shareholders' gala. Tears unexpectedly sprang in Holly's eyes at the artistry of it. She couldn't fathom *ever* needing a dress so fancy.

It was a pearly sky-blue completely covered in hand-sewn crystals. Holly was surprised at how much the gown weighed. Sleeveless with a deep-scooped neck, it skimmed the floor until Diane had her step into coordinating high-heeled sandals.

Whether the dress complemented Holly's icy blue eyes or her eyes enhanced the dress, it didn't matter. There couldn't be a more perfect gown.

She hoped Ethan liked it.

As she stepped into the lounge to model it for him, she wanted to be sure that she was wearing the gown rather than the gown wearing *her.* Standing up straight, with her shoulders back, Holly reminded herself of what she had learned from the posture correction videos that had helped her rid herself of her slump. Stand tall. Ribs over hips. Hips over heels.

She smiled demurely at Ethan as she approached.

He hiccupped as he almost choked on his sip of champagne.

Holly giggled. She high-fived herself in her mind. *Mission accomplished.*

She cooed, high on a unique rush of power she'd never known she had, "Do you still want to marry me?"

Ethan set his champagne flute down on the side table and cleared his throat. "You have no idea…"

"One more stop and then we will go to dinner," Ethan said as he ushered Holly back into the car.

Leonard shut the passenger door, then went around to slide into his place behind the wheel. He deftly maneuvered them away from the curb to join the Fifth Avenue traffic.

Ethan was thinking ahead. "What else do you need for the gala? I assume you would like to have your hair and makeup done?"

"Please."

"I will have Nathan book that."

Holly held her hands up in front of her. There was often a rainbow of colors staining her fingers and nails, but today it was just the Cobalt Two Eleven leftover from last night's spill. "And I think I need a manicure, don't you agree?"

"The way you look in that gown, I doubt anyone would notice."

No fair for him to say things like that. Things that made her want to lean over and cover his luscious lips with an hour-long kiss. Not fair at all for him to speak words that made her contemplate what it would be like to be with someone who made her feel good about herself. Who was on her side.

Not just for business purposes.

Gridlocked traffic was only allowing them to inch forward. The rain had ceased for the moment but the sky was a thick grey. Throngs of pedestrians rushed to and fro. Some darted across the streets, jaywalking quickly in between cars. Horns honked. Drivers yelled at each other. Music blared from taxicab radios. A siren screamed.

Together, it sounded like a riotous symphony. New York was alive and kicking.

One minute she had been crammed into an economy seat on a packed airplane, headed for the Big Apple and who knew what. And then a minute later she was modeling a jewel-encrusted evening gown for a young billionaire.

A smokin' hot young billionaire who had ogled her as if he not only wanted to see those clothes on her, but also wanted to see them in a heap on the floor beside his bed.

By the end of her fashion show Holly had been imagining it as well. How it might feel to have Ethan's big and no doubt able hands unzipping the zippers and unbuttoning the buttons of those finely crafted garments.

How far would it be safe to go with this charade they had embarked on? Surely not as far as clothes being strewn at the bedside.

Holly was going to have to learn to regally accept a peck on the cheek in front of other people without melting into a puddle of desire. She might have to place a reciprocal smooch on Ethan's face at some point. If push came to shove she might even have to receive a kiss on the lips at, say, the shareholders' gala when their engagement was announced.

She had no idea how she'd handle that, but she would cross that bridge when she came to it. However, under no circumstances would her make-believe fiancé's tuxedo—or anything else of his—end up crumpled at the foot of her bed.

No one would ever see them behind closed doors. And she'd do well to remember that to a man like Ethan Benton this was all just a deal. A game. A con. He'd only go as far as was absolutely necessary to do what he deemed right for his aunt Louise's future.

Holly would keep her eye on the prize. A great place to live, steady work, a leg-up for Vince. That was more than she could have ever hoped for. Let alone on her first day here. That was enough. That was astounding.

"Out." Ethan opened the car door in the middle of the street. "This traffic is unbearable. We will go on foot."

"What?"

He firmly grasped Holly's hand and slid them out of the backseat. "Leonard, meet us in front," he instructed, before thumping the door shut. He tugged Holly. "Come on."

"Where are we going?" she asked as he ushered her to the sidewalk.

"I told you. One more stop."

They joined the masses of legs charging north on Fifth Avenue. New Yorkers during rush hour. Always in a hurry. Always somewhere to go. The air was cold. The pace was exhilarating.

Maybe this would become home. Maybe this enthralling city itself would fill up the emptiness she'd always had inside.

Two blocks later she stopped dead in her tracks. They had arrived at their destination. She looked up to take in the majesty of the Art Deco architecture. The bronze sculpture of Atlas holding up the building's clock. The elaborate window displays.

People were moving in and out of the store's entry doors. Many of those leaving held the light blue shopping bags that were known the world over.

"I do not suppose it would do for my fiancée to wear an engagement ring made from a beer bottle wrapper," he said, and winked.

So he hadn't brought her to a jewelry store to get a ring. He'd brought her to *THE* jewelry store.

Ricky had never given her an engagement ring. They'd waited for a sale at the jewelry store in their local mall and bought the two cheapest gold bands there. It had only been last month that she'd gotten around to selling hers for bulk weight to help pay for her plane ticket to New York.

Now she was standing in front of the most well-known jewelry store in the world! Little blue bags!

Inside, Ethan gave his name and they were immediately escorted to the private salon. A man in a pinstriped suit introduced himself as Jeremy Markham.

Again Holly remembered hearing Ethan on the phone that morning with his assistant, Nathan, mentioning a Diane and a Jeremy. Diane was clothes…obviously Jeremy was jewels. Ethan had everything figured out.

"Jeremy, we will need some help with a wardrobe of jewelry in the weeks to come, but today we would like to choose a diamond ring."

"Of course, sir. May I present a selection?"

Ethan nodded.

A private appointment to pick out an engagement ring? Ho-hum, just an ordinary day.

"Please, sit down." Jeremy, chin up high, held a chair out for Holly after giving her a once-over. Like Diane with the clothes, had this salesman who clearly only dealt with VIPs already figured out that Holly was just one big fake? Another opportunist going after a rich man's money.

Using a key extracted from his jacket pocket, Jeremy let himself into a back room.

Ethan pulled a chair next to Holly's.

"Check these out!" she exclaimed at the glass case to the left of them.

A heritage collection of gemstone jewelry was on display. Elaborate necklaces and bracelets made from pounds of gold and carat upon carat of colorful stones. The pieces were too ornate for her taste, but she was attracted to the hues.

What had really caught her eye was a simple ring of blue topaz. The stone was a large oval cut, bordered on each side by two small diamonds.

"Look at how stunning that ring is. That blue is so brilliant it's blinding. Light is bouncing off it in twenty different directions."

Holly's eyes were light blue, like the stone. It had always been her favorite color from as far back as she could remember. Maybe that was why she'd instantly fallen in love with the sky-blue evening gown Ethan had bought for her.

While it had always been pink for girls and blue for boys Holly, as usual, had swum against the stream. It wasn't as if the trailer she'd lived in with her mom and brother had had any décor to it. The walls had been covered in flowery peeling wallpaper. Sheets and blankets had always been chosen by what was on clearance sale, which had usually translated to scratchy fabrics with dark prints. But Holly could remember a few occasions when her father had been in town for a day or so with some money and bought her new clothes. She'd always chosen items in shades of blue.

"It's just dazzling," she continued, pointing to the ring. "I've never seen anything like it."

Ethan glanced over to it and shrugged his shoulders, indifferent.

Jeremy returned with two velvet trays that held a wide variety of ring styles, all with humongous diamonds.

Ethan whispered to Holly, "We ought to be able to find something perfect amongst these."

She shot one final glance at the astounding blue topaz. "Whatever you say. You're the boss…"

"Feng, we will start with hot and sour soup. Follow that with the chef's special duck, beef with broccoli, shrimp chow mein. And oolong tea."

"Thank you, Mr. Ethan." The waiter bowed and hurried away.

After the jewelry store, Ethan had instructed Leonard to drive them to Chinatown. Now he and Holly were comfortably ensconced in a booth at a casual restaurant his family often frequented when they were in New York.

"I am famished," Ethan proclaimed. "Shopping is exhausting."

With a suitably enormous diamond engagement ring now on Holly's finger, the day's checklist was complete. They had been downtown, midtown, and now back downtown, but he was craving familiar food.

"Do you do a lot of shopping?" Holly questioned.

"I suppose I do my fair share, but it is not an activity I have a feeling for one way or another," he lied.

Watching Holly model one comely outfit after another would rank pretty darn high on his list of pleasurable pastimes. Although a lot of his other work had been accomplished today as well, thanks to the convenience of technology. Securing a fiancée had been at the top of his to-do list.

"Do you…" Holly twirled a lock of her raven hair "…shop for women on a regular basis?"

Hmm…fishing, was she?

"Women have dragged me to find gold in China, the finest silks in India, the best leather in Buenos Aires, if that is what you are asking."

She brushed her bangs out of her eyes and sat up straight. "Oh."

The previous women in his life were a sore point with him. In fact Ethan and women had never been a good combination, period. Going all the way back to his mother. Other than Aunt Louise, every woman Ethan had encountered seemed to him to be one hundred percent selfish. Only out for what they could get. Gifts, money, travel, status—you name it.

Which was why he was resolute that he'd never fall in love. To love you had to trust. And that was something he was never going to be tricked into again.

So it was a logical step for him to dream up this scheme that would allow Aunt Louise to think Ethan had found lifelong love as she had with Uncle Mel. Ethan would never have to marry a woman whose motivation he'd question. Intention, compensation and expectation were all upfront with this plan. It might be the brainiest partnership deal he'd ever conceived.

"Hot and sour soup." Feng placed the steaming bowl on the table. While he ladled out two servings he questioned, "May I ask if Mrs. Louise is feeling better?"

His aunt Louise had been in New York several times in the past few months. Feng had probably seen her more recently than Ethan had.

"Was she unwell when she was last here?"

The waiter pursed his lips and bowed his head, which said more than any words could.

Ethan's heart sank. This validated the fact that he was on the right track. Doing whatever it took to get Aunt Louise to retire and relax in Barbados before worse things than stumbles and bruises stole her dignity.

It was all going to work out.

As long as Ethan continued to stare past but not into Holly Motta's face. Because when he did steal a glance she didn't look like a business proposition. Or a gold-digger out to get what she deemed hers. With that slouch she kept correcting, and that milky skin, and the hint of ache in her eyes…

No, she was a living, breathing, kindred spirit who could shred his master plan into a million slices if he wasn't careful.

"Why are you looking at me like that?" she asked with her spoon in the air.

"Like what?" Ethan threw back his head with an exaggerated nonchalance.

She gave him a mock frown.

"Eat your soup," he told her.

One very ungenteel slurp later… *"Yummo!"*

"We should learn more about each other if we are to be convincing as a couple. You clearly like food."

He mocked her slurp until they were both laughing.

"My turn," she said. "You're an only child."

"You have one brother."

"You studied at Oxford."

"What is your favorite movie?"

Holly dismissed him with a wave of her hand. "Are you kidding me? If we're going to get to know each other we have to get real. What is the one thing that has hurt you the most in your life?"

His mother. Of course it was his mother. Nothing could

devastate a nine-year-old boy more than being left behind by his mother. It was horrible enough that his father had died instantly when a drunk driver had plowed into his car at racing speed, killing him instantly. But then shortly after that to lose his mother in the way he had… It was unthinkable.

"Beef with snow peas. Shrimp chow mein. Chef's special duck," Feng announced as he and another waiter positioned the platters in the center of the table. "Please enjoy."

Saved by the duck.

Ethan wasn't going to expose his darkness and despair to someone he'd met only yesterday. As a matter of fact he wasn't in the habit of talking about his feelings with *anyone*. It was better that way.

He scooped a portion of each dish onto his and Holly's plates.

But wasn't it rather amazing that this woman was so genuine she didn't want to discuss trivial matters?

As she lifted her chopsticks to grab at her chow mein he admired the diamond ring he had put on her finger. It was staggering in its size and clarity, and he knew any woman would be filled with pride to wear something so timeless and flawless.

Yet he could kick himself because he hadn't bought her the blue topaz ring she had admired at the store!

Quick thinking had told him to buy the type of ring that was expected of him. Anything other than a traditional diamond engagement ring would invite inquiry. Such as where and why and what sentiments had inspired him to buy such an unusual ring. Those were extra questions they didn't need. It would just add to the risk of them flubbing up as a believable couple.

But now he thought blue ring, purple ring, green ring— what would it matter if that was what she wanted?

Pulsing and vibrant, Holly Motta had careened into his apartment with blue paint on her face and, he feared, had changed his life forever. Forcing him to think about women differently than he ever had. Making him for the first time vaguely envision a role in which he cared if someone was happy. Edging him into speculation about what it would be like if someone cared about his happiness, too.

And now she was making it hard to concentrate on anything other than leaping across the table and planting a kiss on that sweet mouth that was busy with noodles.

After a bite of food to steady himself, Ethan resumed their interview. "Tell me something about yourself that I would not have guessed."

"I used to be—" she blurted, and then abruptly stopped herself. She put her chopsticks down and took a slow sip of her tea. Trying to recover, she finished with, "A pretty good softball player."

Aha, so it wasn't as easy for her to be as open and candid as she wanted him to believe it was. What had she been about to say that had proved too difficult to reveal? And what had she avoided telling him at breakfast that morning about the mother she'd characterized as *unpredictable*?

He'd gone along with her easy sincerity, but Ethan really didn't know the first thing about her. He'd garnered that she'd had a difficult childhood, but it wasn't like him to take anyone at face value. Not after what he'd seen of life.

Guard and defend.

He had his family's empire to protect.

"Excuse me," he said as he put his chopsticks down and pulled out his phone. "I have just remembered one more bit of business for the day."

He texted Chip Foley, Benton Worldwide's Head of Security. Just as he'd intended to do if he'd hired an actress for the fiancée job.

Chip, please run everything you can on a Holly Motta from Fort Pierce, Florida. Claims her occupation is artist. I would place her age at about thirty. Tall, slim, blue eyes, black hair. She says her brother Vince works for us in Miami. I do not know if it is the same last name. Do an across-the-board check on her for me.

After hitting the "send" button, his eyes returned to Holly.

She pointed her chopsticks at him and taunted, "Hey, you never told me what it was in your life that hurt you the most."

CHAPTER SIX

IT WAS THE dead of night, but Holly could still hear New York outside the bedroom window. Cars drove by. A dog barked. People laughed boisterously on the street.

The city that never slept.

Lying in Ethan's bed, with her head sinking into his soft pillows, she could hardly make sense of the day. Visiting Soho galleries, buying all those art supplies, a new wardrobe, a diamond ring... Then that dinner in Chinatown.

She'd lived a lifetime in the last twenty-four hours.

Ethan was just beyond the door in the living room. Was he sleeping? Was he working? Or was he lying awake thinking about her as she was of him?

Of course not, Holly reminded herself. Ethan Benton had more important things on his mind then his wife for hire. She'd better remember that.

But when they'd watched each other's faces at the restaurant it had seemed as if maybe she would, in fact, linger in his thoughts and keep him up at night. He'd looked at her as if there was nowhere else he'd rather be. The restaurant might have been crowded and clamoring, but he'd never taken his eyes off her.

Through most of the evening they would have convinced anyone they were an engaged couple. Finishing each other's sentences… Digging their chopsticks into each other's plates…

And then there had been those awkward moments when they'd asked each other questions neither was ready to answer.

Holly hadn't been able to bring herself to tell Ethan that she had been married. She feared he would think of her as a used product and not want to go through with their agreement. He didn't need to know about her mistake in marrying someone who hadn't loved her for who she was. Who hadn't supported the person she wanted to become. Ricky Dowd wasn't a name that *ever* needed to come up in conversation.

They would go through with their pretend engagement so that Ethan could protect his aunt as her health declined. And, as he'd said, either they would continue to meet for official occasions or eventually call off their deal. Whatever happened, Ethan would never have to know about Holly's wasted time on wrong decisions that tonight seemed like a million years ago.

Just as she might not find out what he was hiding because he didn't want to tell her what had caused him the most hurt in his life. It had to be something terrible, because both times when he'd avoided the topic his eyes had turned to coal.

But the rest of the evening was a dream she never wanted to wake from. When they had got to unimportant questions, like favorite movies and television shows, they'd laughed themselves dizzy remembering jokes from silly comedies. Laughed some more about bad childhood haircuts and mean teachers they'd hated in school.

They had stayed long after the restaurant had emptied, until the staff had been ready to leave. Feng had walked them out to the street and waved them goodbye as they'd tucked themselves into the car so Leonard could deposit them home.

Holly drifted off to sleep, replaying over and over again how Ethan had gently kissed the back of her hand and thanked her for an unforgettable day before he closed the bedroom door.

In the morning, Ethan scrutinized his unshaven face in the bathroom mirror. He hadn't laughed as much as he had last night in a long time. Truth be told, he couldn't remember ever laughing that much. Everything was full power with Holly. Near her, he felt alive with a liquid fire.

That might burn down his life as he knew it.

After showering and dressing, he charted a direct route into the kitchen toward the coffeepot.

"Morning," she greeted him.

"Yes."

He was careful not to touch her as he crossed behind her in the tiny kitchen to pour a cup. It took stupendous will not to reach for her, to put his arms around her waist and find out what her hair might smell like if his face was buried in it.

Instead, more guarding and defending.

He gained distance by busying himself with checking the morning's urgencies on his tablet. His approval was needed on important architectural specifications for the Jersey City project. An email chain between several of the interested parties provided updates. Thank heavens for work. He needed the interruption from his growing and wholly off-track desires for more than what he'd signed up for with Holly.

Despite his efforts, his eyes of their own volition kept darting upward from the screen as he watched her lay out a light breakfast of toast and juice.

"Right, then, we have an important day," he directed

as soon as they'd sat down with their food. "Aunt Louise and Fernando will arrive at six o'clock. She does not like to stay out late in the evening. We should have dinner on the table by seven."

"I made a shopping list," Holly reported. "I'll go to the store, then get the pot roast into the slow cooker."

"I have several meetings today. Can you manage the shopping on your own?"

She snickered. "I've been doing the grocery shopping since I was seven years old. I think I can handle a New York City supermarket."

"I am the one who would have trouble."

"But after that I'll need you for the painting. I have the canvas size I want. And I'll use acrylic so it will dry quickly. We'll hang it later this afternoon, and no one will be any the wiser that I only painted it today."

With a busy day ahead, he'd selectively forgotten that he had agreed to her doing a painting of him. He had no time for posing. Although a painting by her would be a very eye-catching and convincing symbol that they were really a couple.

Plus, it would put him in proximity with her from midday. Which he had to admit he'd be looking forward to.

He mentally reprimanded himself for that thought.

In front of the building, Ethan watched Holly walk down the block while Leonard held the car door open for him. Her glossy hair swung to and fro. It was another gloomy day, but dry at the moment. Her jeans and that black leather jacket she seemed to favor would be sufficient for her shopping trip. Why he was concerned with how she was dressed for the weather was baffling. And disturbing.

But what would a Florida girl know about winter? She might catch cold...

Leonard ferried him from one appointment to the next. The low-income housing project in the Bronx was behind schedule and over budget. He pored over blueprints with the architect until they found a way to enlarge the kitchens for the exterior-facing units. The architect was feuding with the contractor over the selection of materials, but that always seemed to be the case. Ethan was able to smooth some ruffled feathers.

He stopped at the hotel where the shareholders' gala would be held on Saturday. Gave his authorization for the layout of the ballroom. Visualizing the room full of formally dressed people, he could picture them raising their champagne glasses as Aunt Louise offered a toast to him and Holly. His bride-to-be would charm the crowd with her engaging smile and shimmering gown...

In the silence of the empty ballroom, Ethan's heart pleaded for something he couldn't fully grasp. A dull ache thudded in the center of his chest.

Swiftly shoving those confusing feelings aside, he hurried out through the hotel doors to Leonard's car and his next meeting.

The multi-use development in Chelsea had come a long way since he'd last seen it. As he strode through he offered dozens of hellos to the many workers laboring on the project's five buildings. It was for this large venture that he'd offered Holly the commission to do the artwork. The opportunity that had sealed the negotiations for her to agree to pose as his fiancée.

Ethan's interior designer had been intrigued to hear about the up-and-coming artist from Florida he had brought onto the job. He had provided Stella with Holly's website address.

Midday, he returned to the apartment. Holly must not have had any trouble with the slow cooker, because the aroma of cooking meat practically had him salivating.

"My, my..." he said as he removed his coat and hung it on the rack.

The open area by the living room window had been turned into a temporary artist's studio.

"I've been working."

"I can see."

The easel they had bought yesterday was unpacked and in use. A side table with a tarp thrown over it for protection had become a paint station. Another tarp covered the area's floor.

"What have you done with my apartment?"

"Hey, I thought it was *my* apartment."

"Tonight it will be *our* apartment."

"Don't worry. I'll clean it all up after I do the painting of you."

"What do we have here?"

Three pastel drawings on paper lay on the floor. Moving vehicles was their theme. One was a bright yellow taxi done in abstracted horizontal lines that made it look as if it was in motion. Ditto for a blue city bus motoring along. And likewise for a silver train car that appeared to be whizzing by.

"I was working out some ideas. Will there be a valet and transportation station at the Chelsea development?"

Of course. He nodded with immediate understanding. Paintings like this would be stylish and hip, and convey the movement of the city. They'd be perfect. Even if their marriage arrangement proved to be the wrong move, Ethan was at least sure he'd hired an artist who would produce what he needed for the multi-million-dollar project.

"Excellent."

"We'd better not waste any time. When can you be ready to sit for me?"

A grin tried to crack at his mouth. "Let me just wash up. Dinner smells delicious."

Minutes later, he stepped onto the tarp of her studio area.

"I am ready for you," he said bravely, with arms out-stretched.

In reality, he didn't know what to expect. Was not at all comfortable with how Holly might portray him. He reminded himself that this was ultimately for the good of Aunt Louise. He could put up with a little uneasiness for the sake of her wellbeing.

"I'll have you sitting on the stool." Holly, all business, gestured for him to take his place.

She studied him intently. Backed away to get one perspective. Inched to the side for another. Then came in close. So close he could feel the heat of her body, which made him want to do anything *but* sit still.

"What are you deciding on?"

"The perspective. I think I'll do it at an angle that's a partial profile."

"Will it be only my face?"

She ran a finger across his upper chest from shoulder to shoulder to illustrate the cut-off point. Blood pumped double-time to every inch of him she touched. He instinctively leaned away.

"Don't worry. I won't bite."

His voice came out a jagged growl. "It was not you I was worried about."

She smiled quizzically for several beats. His chest muscles continued to vibrate from her touch.

It occurred to him that for all the questions they'd asked each other about favorite things and childhood memories, they hadn't talked about past relationships.

Had a man broken her heart? Had she broken someone's? Was she looking for love?

Did she wonder about him?

Love wasn't on the bargaining table in their business deal. He'd never loved. Didn't love. Wouldn't love. That was a contract signed a long time ago.

Holly programmed some upbeat music into her phone and began. She wanted to do a preliminary pencil drawing on paper, and when she was satisfied with that move on to paint and canvas.

With a last adjustment to his angle, she requested, "Try not to move."

"Do I need to be silent?"

"I'll let you know when I'm sketching your mouth. Just keep your head still when you talk."

With his face turned toward the window, it was odd to feel her eyes on him when he couldn't see her face. Odd, but spine-tingling. And erotic. He wished he could rip off his clothes and have her paint him in the nude.

Holly made him want to let go of the well-bred and well-mannered businessman he was. With her, he wanted to howl naked under the moonlight. And to ravage her with the savage passion he kept tightly caged inside him.

"Can you soften your facial expression?" she asked, making him realize that he was not masking his arousal.

He neutralized his jaw.

"Tell me about your morning," she coaxed.

He appreciated her trying to help him relax. "There are ongoing issues with my housing development in the Bronx. I want to build the maximum number of comfortable units on the property to give as many families as possible a home of their own."

"What are the problems?"

"Materials are costly. I have shareholders to answer to. And Aunt Louise. I promised this as a break-even project—not one on which the company would lose a lot of money. I may have to move it into the category of charitable endeavor. I will have to present it accordingly. Tricky."

"Here, take a look." Holly unclipped from the easel the large piece of paper she'd been using for her sketch and held it up in front of her for him to see.

After preparing himself to hate it, he saw that it wasn't bad at all. She'd used those same short lines she had on the transportation drawings. Together, the strokes formed the likeness of a pensive man looking into the distance.

Holly's face was flushed. She was nervously waiting for his reaction.

With a voice tight and caught, she squeaked, "What do you think?"

"Is this how I look?"

"Well, obviously you're handsome. I hoped I could convey your seriousness, too."

She'd said "handsome" as matter-of-factly as it would have been to say he was wearing a white shirt. He liked it that she thought he was handsome.

"I suppose I am serious."

"That feels like your core. You're formal. You're measured."

"Whereas *you* just say or do anything that comes into your mind."

"And you don't seem like someone who ever loses control."

Oh, if she only knew the thoughts he was having about grabbing her and showing her exactly how out of control he could be.

She was uncovering wild ideas in him. Holly, with her mesmerizing black hair and sinewy limbs. He'd stripped open more of his true self to her in the last two days than he had with anyone in his life. Not all his secrets, but he'd revealed a lot.

And he must rein that in right now. She only needed to know what was relevant to their phony engagement. Nothing more.

He stood up from his stool to stretch and take a break. Checked messages on his phone. Fired off a couple of texts.

Using a sketchpad, Holly quickly drew more versions

of his mouth until she was satisfied. Then showed him the one that she liked.

"Interesting… It looks as if it is easy enough for you to make a small correction here and there and come out with a quite different result."

She shrugged her shoulders. "I guess so. Trial and error."

"I would not have a clue how to do that."

"I'll show you sometime."

"I would like that."

How absurd this was—letting someone sketch his mouth. In the middle of a workday. When he had a thousand other things on his mind.

But he didn't care. Inexplicably, he wanted to be near Holly. She'd definitely cast a spell on him.

She lifted a large canvas onto her easel and adjusted the height. Then picked out her first brush.

"I'm ready to paint. Let's begin."

"Holly Motta, this is my aunt, Louise Benton." Ethan made the introduction as soon as he'd ushered in the visitors.

With a welcoming smile Holly shook the older lady's hand. "I'm happy to finally meet you. I've heard so much about you."

"And I so little about you…" Louise assessed her. "How pretty you are, dear."

"I'd say the same about you. Let Ethan take your coat."

Holly reminded herself to stay focused in spite of her nerves. At this moment her end of the contract had come due. Louise had to be convinced beyond a shadow of a doubt that not only was she Ethan's true love, but that he had made the right choice in her.

As Ethan helped his aunt to remove her coat Louise almost lost her balance. A telltale sign of her medical condition. How difficult living with a chronic problem like that must be. Still, Louise had style despite her petite and frail frame. A sheet of thin white hair curled under at her shoulders…her simple dark green dress was the picture of good taste.

She was the type of accomplished woman Holly looked up to. Holly was glad she had chosen to wear the black trousers and gray blouse from the new clothes Ethan had bought her. Even though it was dinner at home, these were not people who dined in jeans.

"Such an unusual silver necklace…" Holly initiated conversation.

Louise looked to Ethan. "Yes, my dear nephew brought it back from…remind me where it was from?"

"Turkey."

"Yes, Istanbul. Ethan always brings me unique trinkets from his travels."

With Louise's head turned toward Ethan, Holly noticed the large bruise across her cheekbone. That must have been from the fall Ethan had said she'd taken last week. Holly understood his wish to shield his aunt from the public eye, with her decline so visible.

"Huh…low…oh…" Louise's husband, Fernando, finally insisted on being acknowledged. Ethan hadn't yet taken his coat, and nor had an introduction been made.

"Yes, Fernando Layne—meet my fiancée, Holly Motta."

"Charmed," Fernando replied, without extending his hand.

"Nice to meet you." Holly rocked back on her heels, unsure how to move on if they weren't going to shake hands.

"Are we having cocktails?" Fernando flung his coat to Ethan.

"Let me mix you something," Ethan offered.

"I know where the drinks are." Fernando rebuffed him and headed to the liquor cabinet.

Ethan had told Holly it was Fernando who had bought

this apartment. On behalf of Benton Worldwide and with the company's money, of course. And that he made frequent shopping trips to New York.

Forty-five years old trying to look twenty-five, judging from his slicked-back hair and skinny pants. No doubt Fernando preferred chic New York to less flashy Boston, although Holly couldn't say for sure having never been there. But in an instant she knew that she wouldn't trust Fernando if her life depended on it.

"Louise." Fernando presented his wife with a glass of brown liquor.

She refused. "You know I'm not drinking with the new medications," she said.

"A sparkling water, then." He took the glass and drank it in one tip, then scurried back to the bar to pour Louise some water. Not asking if Holly and Ethan wanted anything.

Fernando's eye caught the painting of Ethan, now on the wall where those impersonal black and white photos had been. "You two have certainly settled in."

Holly bit her lip. *If he only knew.* About her barging in on Ethan just two days ago... That this apartment Fernando thought was his had become part of Ethan and Holly's agreement... How no one in this room knew that her feelings for Ethan were becoming closer to real rather than the masquerade they were meant to be...

"Did you do this, my dear?" Louise moved toward the painting to take a closer look.

It had turned out well, especially for only an afternoon's work. It was all done in blue—a tribute to the paint color she'd had on her face and hands when she had first rushed into this apartment, expecting it to be empty.

She'd probably had more fun than she should have painting Ethan. What an impressive subject he was. With his upright posture. Finely chiseled jaw. The deep, deep eyes with just a hint of crinkle at the outer corners. And his mouth! That mouth! No wonder it had taken her a few sketches until she got it right. Lips not so full as to be feminine. Lips she longed to explore with her own, not with her paintbrush…

"The first of many to come, I hope." Holly slipped her arm through Ethan's in a way she thought a fiancée in love might. His muscles jumped, but at least he didn't bristle and pull away. "Ethan's not keen on sitting for me."

"He never was," Louise agreed. "Didn't we have to bribe you with sweets in order to get you to stay still for those Christmas portraits every year?"

"I told Holly about that crotchety old painter who smelled of pipe tobacco. She is lucky I was not scarred for life."

Conversational banter. *Check*. This couldn't be going better.

"I see you captured that distinctive curl of hair over Ethan's forehead," Louise noted.

That curl had captured Holly—not the other way around. The magnificent way his wavy hair spilled over in front. Just a little bit. Just enough…

It was the one thing that wasn't completely tamed and restrained about Ethan. Somehow that curl hinted at the fiery, emotional man she knew lay beneath the custom-made suits and the multi-million-dollar deals.

"I certainly never learned how to paint or draw," Ethan said, with a convincingly proud smile of approval at his fiancée's handiwork.

While they chatted about the painting Fernando moseyed over to Ethan's desk. Out of the corner of her eye, Holly saw him snooping at the papers on top of it.

Fernando was making himself a bit too much at home. Funny that Holly felt territorial after only two days. She knew that Fernando used this apartment frequently. But he didn't keep any of his personal possessions here because other employees and associates of Benton Worldwide also used it when they were in New York.

Still, she didn't think Fernando had the right to be looking at anything Ethan might have put down on the desk. But it wasn't her place to say anything.

"Louise, would you like to sit down at the table?" Holly suggested.

She took Louise's elbow and guided her toward the dining area. Ethan and Fernando followed suit behind them.

Holly overheard Fernando hiss to Ethan, "I know what you're up to. You've found a wife so that Louise will retire and you can take over. If you think I'm going to spend the rest of her life getting sunburned on a boring island, you've got another think coming."

CHAPTER SEVEN

"SO FAR SO GOOD," Holly said as she placed four plates on the kitchen counter so that she and Ethan could begin to serve dinner.

"Except that I had forgotten how much I detest that little Fernando," he retorted.

Holly was only playing the role of soon-to-be member of this unusual family. She shouldn't be privy to the disagreements and resentments that might lie beneath the surface. So it wouldn't be proper for her to ask Ethan what Fernando had meant about not wanting to move to Barbados when Louise retired. Obviously the comment had made Ethan mad.

She removed the lid of the slow cooker. "Where did they meet?"

Speaking in a hushed voice, because Aunt Louise and her man-toy weren't far away at the dining table, Ethan explained. "Our office manager at Headquarters hired him. His title is 'Client Relations Coordinator,' or some such nonsense. He does scarcely more than order fancy coffees for meetings and come here to New York or go to Europe to spend the company's money. Of course I cannot fire him." Ethan gritted his teeth. "As much as I would like to."

With serving utensils, Holly lifted hearty chunks of the pot roast onto each plate. Ethan reached in with a fork to assist her. They worked seamlessly as a team, anticipating each other's moves. Now pros at navigating the square footage of the small kitchen.

"What does she see in him?"

"Companionship. I suppose he makes her feel younger. She was devastated after Uncle Mel died."

"She must miss Mel horribly."

"They were a partnership in more ways than I can count. Not being able to have children brought them even closer. Taking me in was another thing they did together."

With Ethan having witnessed such a solid marriage between his aunt and uncle, Holly wondered why he was so adamant that he himself would never marry for love. What had happened to close him off to the possibility?

Ethan ladled mashed potatoes while Holly spooned gravy on top. "So Fernando has been able to fill the hole left by your uncle's death?"

"Hardly. He could *never* step into my uncle's shoes. But I will grant that he provides a diversion. Within a year of Uncle Mel's death Aunt Louise began having symptoms of this hereditary neuropathy that she remembers her mother suffering from."

"Losing your husband and developing an illness, one after the other. That's awful."

"She could have sunk into a depression. Fernando at least gives her something to do. He keeps her busy with Boston society dinners and parties on Cape Cod. He will do the same in Barbados. I will remind him that *I* am the boss as often as I need to. We know a lot of people there. He can develop a social calendar for her."

"Give her things to look forward to?"

"Yes. Without children, there are no grandchildren on the horizon. Although I suppose she assumes you and I will have…" He trailed off.

Children. With Ethan.

The mere thought halted Holly in place. A home of her own. Filled with noise and food and laughter and love. Beautiful toddlers running around with reddish-brown tufts of hair falling onto their foreheads. Tall Ethan reaching down to hold little hands.

Did he ever think about having children?

He'd frozen too, holding a spoon in his hand, also lost in contemplation. Was he picturing the same thing?

He'd be a good father. The way he put so much care and thought into his aunt and what was best for her was like the devotion and concern she had for Vince, having practically raised her brother single-handedly because her mother had proved incapable. She had more of that kind of love to give.

Someday.

It wasn't going to be now.

That was much further far down the line. If ever.

No, this current arrangement was ideal. A new life for herself in New York. Not being pulled down by other people. Putting herself first. Free at last.

Everything was upfront with Ethan. There was zero chance of her being hurt. Zero love. Zero disappointment. So he was intelligent and intense? And gorgeous? That was ultimately irrelevant to the duties at hand. They were two professionals, doing their jobs.

Holly used tongs to crown each dinner plate with roasted carrots. Forging ahead. Although she wished her fingernails weren't spotted with paint.

"We did it. Dinner is served."

As she carried two plates to the dining table, she saw Fernando's hand atop of Louise's. The older woman's face did seem to have a livelier blush with his attention on her. Even if Fernando's intentions were less than honorable, Holly could understand the purpose he filled. Life was all about compromises.

Ethan brought the other two plates. While he poured water she ducked back into the kitchen for rolls and butter before sitting to eat.

"Holly, this is delicious," Louise proclaimed.

"I'm glad you like it. You sound surprised?"

"Indeed. I don't know that Ethan has ever dated a woman before who would know how to make an old-fashioned pot roast."

Ethan leaned to pat Holly's arm. She smiled at the unspoken compliment, as a fiancée should. "Aunt Louise, I have never dated a woman who has likely ever eaten pot roast, let alone prepared it."

"Where did you learn to cook like this?"

"I took a course in cooking classic American comfort food," Holly fibbed, without missing a beat. Louise didn't need to know that if she hadn't taught herself to cook she and Vince wouldn't have eaten. "I'll have to make cheeseburgers for you next time."

"Now, Ethan, dear," Louise said, "you have been keeping your delightful lady a secret. You must tell us everything about where and how you met," she insisted.

Fernando buttered a roll and gobbled it down.

Holly and Ethan, the happy couple, gazed lovingly at each other as if to signal that they were off and running. They'd been rehearsing. Now they'd be put to the test.

"Aunt Louise, I wanted to be absolutely sure of myself before I said anything to you," Ethan began. "Holly's brother is Vince Motta. He works for us in the Miami office."

Aunt Louise listened attentively as she continued eating. Fernando chomped on chunks of meat that he yanked off his fork with his lower teeth.

"It was at the groundbreaking ceremony for the Coconut Grove project," Holly continued. For accuracy, Ethan had filled her in on the details of that luncheon. "We were both reaching for the same shrimp on the buffet table. Our hands touched."

"And it was magic."

Ethan fluttered his eyelashes, which made Holly giggle.

She'd visualized this fairy tale over and over—to the point that now she would have sworn it had actually happened. The elegant outdoor celebration... Her in a pink dress, talking to her brother, Vince, and a couple of his coworkers... After excusing herself she left them to explore the lavish seafood table. And just as she reached for the plumpest, juiciest-looking shrimp on the tray a hand from the opposite direction nabbed the same one.

She tugged on her end of the shrimp, the other hand on the other end, until their fingers intertwined.

They turned to look at each other.

He surrendered the crustacean.

The skies parted.

The angels cascaded down from heaven playing trumpets.

"It was love at first shrimp..." They sighed in unison.

"How romantic." Louise was sufficiently charmed.

"We talked for hours that afternoon." Ethan laid it on thick. "But then I had to board a plane for Bangkok."

"We didn't see each other again for months."

Caught up in their "reminiscing," they moved their faces toward each other. Involuntarily. As if pulled together by a magnet.

Ethan bent in and brought his mouth to Holly's. Only it wasn't a feather-soft fake dinner kiss, meant to convince his aunt. No, his unexpected lips were bold. And hot. And they smashed against hers.

Their insistence didn't let her pull away. She swirled inside. Got lost in the moment. Let it go on several beats too many.

Until she could finally separate herself from him.

Holly feared that everyone at the table could hear her heart pounding outside her chest.

Ethan looked as shocked as she felt. But after a moment he picked up his fork and resumed eating. Following his lead, she did the same.

Fortunately neither Louise nor Fernando had noticed anything strange. Holly and Ethan were engaged, after all. Why *wouldn't* they spontaneously kiss?

But he wasn't helping her any with a kiss like that. Let that be a warning to her.

Louise inquired, "Are your people from Miami, dear?"

Holly barely had a moment to catch her breath—nowhere near enough time to recover from that inebriating kiss before there came the next flaming hoop she had to jump through. She didn't have "people." And the people she did have she needed to keep a secret. Her people were not Benton kind of people.

"No. Fort Pierce."

"Fort *Pierce*?" Fernando tossed back.

Certainly not the kind of stylish metropolis full of chic hotels, South Beach beauties and all-night parties that would interest him.

"We met again last year here in New York, when Holly was exhibiting paintings at a Soho gallery," Ethan fibbed to move their story forward.

"Then wasn't the next time when you came down and we visited Key West?"

He leaned over to brush the side of her cheek with the back of his hand. "It was then that I knew for sure."

His tender touch across Holly's face made it a struggle to keep her eyes open. Especially after that not so gentle kiss had rocked her to the bone.

Ethan sensed he had made her uncomfortable. "More water, anyone?" he said quickly, refilling glasses without waiting for an answer.

Thankfully giving her a moment to regroup.

After a couple of quiet sips Holly ventured, "I'm so happy we're finally together in New York. I haven't been here in five years."

Ethan, Louise and Fernando all looked at her.

Oh, no! Oh! No!

Fernando's eyes narrowed. "I thought you said you had a painting exhibition here last year?"

Gulp. Ethan's soft stroke to her face had thrown her off course. Let her talk before she thought.

Dead silence. Which was finally broken by the sound of a fax coming in on Ethan's desk.

"I meant that I haven't explored the city in years." Holly took a shot. "That was a work trip. I hardly left the gallery."

"Shall we have dessert?" Ethan did his best to defuse the moment.

"Let me help you, dear." Louise slowly rose and followed Ethan into the kitchen.

Fernando kept his glare on Holly one uncomfortable moment longer before he shot up to strut to the liquor cabinet.

Left at the table, Holly stood and began clearing the dishes. Not knowing how badly she had messed things up. Whether Ethan would be furious with her or sympathetic over her flub. Unsure if anyone had bought her quick cover-up.

Louise, even with her reduced ability, had offered to help Ethan with dessert in the kitchen. She must want to say something to him that she didn't want Holly to hear.

Careful not to interrupt Ethan and his aunt's private conversation, she stacked the dirty plates and brushed crumbs off the table. The dessert dishes and silverware were on a side shelf, so she set those out.

The evening had been going so nicely. Louise seemed

to like her. Hopefully Holly hadn't unraveled everything with one slip of the tongue.

With each passing minute Holly had come to like the idea of being Ethan's pretend fiancée more and more. She wanted to make this work. To have the art commission and a place to live. It was a peculiar arrangement, for sure, but a better starting point for a new life than she could ever have imagined. At almost thirty, it was time for her to rewind and reboot. Put the bad choices—Ricky—and the bad luck—her mother—behind her.

When Ethan had sweetened the deal by agreeing to use his influence to help her brother, Vince, get a promotion, Holly had had to roll the dice and give it a try. Ethan had said he couldn't make any promises, but Holly knew Vince was a hard and devoted worker who could easily manage additional responsibilities. She'd never forgive herself if her mistake tonight had done anything to endanger his chances of success.

And, *wow*, she was going to have to lay down some ground rules about her physical interactions with Ethan. She was shocked at how she was drawn to him almost hypnotically, easily touching his arm and lightly laying a hand on the small of his back as if it was no big deal. Like a fiancée would.

But that kiss had shown her how quickly things could go too far. His mouth on hers had dizzied her, made her lose track of her thoughts, forget the company she was in. Ethan's lips were dangerous weapons. They could completely daze her, leave her woozy and unable to do the job he had hired her for.

What she needed was to figure out a system whereby his touch had no effect on her. She'd work that out. This *was* playacting, after all.

The dessert and coffee dishes set, an odd sight greeted Holly when she turned around from the table. Fernando was again in front of Ethan's desk. This time he was peering at the fax they had just heard come through. His eyes widened and he snatched the piece of paper from the machine, folded it and slid it into his pocket. Not noticing that Holly was watching.

Because Fernando supposedly spent a lot of time in this apartment, the fax might be something he was expecting. But it irked her that he was again hovering around the paperwork and personal items that Ethan had spread out on the desk. However, she didn't know all the facts. He was Louise's husband. She couldn't question him even though she wanted to. She was a hired hand who didn't know what went on in this family.

She had already screwed up. Her job right now was to keep her nose down. And do her best to salvage the rest of the evening.

Ethan's arm around Holly's shoulder, they said goodbye to Louise and Fernando as the elevator door closed.

Back in the apartment, Ethan clenched his fist in victory. "Success!"

"Do you think everything went all right? I was so worried. And then I bungled up about not having spent time in New York."

"You recovered. Aunt Louise adored you instantly."

"She did?"

"In the kitchen she told me she could tell right away that you had good character and were not out for our money or the family name."

"If she only knew…"

Ethan mused on that truth.

Together they cleared the remains of the apple crisp and cinnamon-flavored coffee. The kitchen looked as if they had just fed a hundred people. Dirty pots and pans were strewn on every available surface. The sink was stacked with plates. Spills puddled on the countertops.

"I will pay the housekeeper triple to clean this tomorrow!" Ethan said.

"Do you want to go out?" Holly asked.

"Out? Right now?"

"Yes. It's not that late. And I'm full of nervous energy."

Ethan contemplated the idea. Aunt Louise had started to tire so easily the dinner had been over even earlier than expected. "Where would you like to go?"

"Show me some of the Benton buildings in New York."

He whipped out his phone.

Ten minutes later they were curbside as Leonard pulled up in the town car. It was a dry but very cold evening. Holly wore that favorite black leather jacket, and looked utterly lovable with a red beanie, scarf and gloves. Ethan didn't bring a hat, but dressed warmly with his own brown leather jacket and wool scarf.

Once they'd pulled away from the building Ethan recited to Leonard a quick list of addresses and the tour commenced. As usual, his driver maneuvered the car deftly through the always-present Manhattan traffic.

Holly had had the right idea. The crisp night was invigorating.

Or maybe *she* was the cause of the vigor he felt.

She had played her part to a tee at dinner, and he was sure Aunt Louise suspected nothing of his ruse. How fragile his dearly loved aunt had looked tonight. With those bruises on her face from the tumble she'd taken—in front of employees, no less—at Benton headquarters.

He plugged a reminder into his phone to hire an expert makeup artist for the gala.

But a nagging complication had plagued him throughout dinner. Nothing about the evening had felt fake. Everything had come naturally. From their comfortable banter to the way he and Holly had served the food together and the electrifying kiss they'd shared while telling the story of how they met.

Moment after moment had passed when he had almost forgotten this was a charade. Worse still, the feeling had filled him with a jarring elation and contentment.

This was new territory and it petrified him. He'd never given serious thought to a real-life real wife, and now was not the time to start. Concentrating on moving Aunt Louise into retirement and moving the company into a more charitable direction was plenty for the foreseeable future. Plus, he had vowed long ago never to be swayed into forgetting one critical fact.

Women were not to be trusted.

Aunt Louise was the only exception in his life. Didn't he know that well enough?

All—and that meant *all*—the women he had ever dated had betrayed him. Society girls, daughters of noblemen and businesswomen alike. They might have approached him as a colleague. Or cozied up to him as the wholesome girl-next-door. Others had come on stronger and seduced him with sexual wiles.

Not that he hadn't gone along with them.

He'd satisfied his urges. Indulged in temptations.

Several of them quite memorable.

Yes, maybe a few of them had made him imagine going past three dates or three weeks. But in the end they had always showed their true colors. They hadn't been who they'd said they were. Even some of their body parts hadn't been real. They had all been something other than what they had seemed. Out for something. A piece of *him*.

And his mother—his own mother—had been the worst offender of them all. That a woman could turn her back on her own son for personal gain was a hurt he'd do well to remember for the rest of his life. Apparently women were capable of the unthinkable.

So, even though his aunt sensed that Holly's intentions were good, he mustn't forget that they were performing in a play. All he could really know was that Holly was a competent actress. Instinct told him that this enchanting woman had a kind heart and honorable aims. But he'd only known her for a couple of days. She might prove herself to be just like the others. And there was plenty she could be hiding. Ethan hadn't received the background probe from his security chief yet.

"This is the Seventy-Fourth Street development we did about a decade ago." He pointed out the window when they reached their first destination. "Leonard, can you pull over to the curb?"

Lit from within, the gleaming glass tower shot upward into the night sky. Ethan leaned close to Holly, beside him in the backseat, to show off some details.

"We did the first story with a wider base, and then the remaining twenty-nine floors in a slender tower coming up in the middle. The larger platform of the first level allows for greenery to encircle building."

"Is the first-story garden accessible?" Holly asked, wide-eyed.

"Yes. It was designed so that employees in the offices can go outside into green space whenever they want."

Their next destination was Forty-First Street.

"This one is over twenty-five years old. It was the last project my father worked on before he died. Here they had the issue of erecting new construction in between two buildings from the nineteen-thirties," he explained.

"New York is amazing like that, isn't it?" Holly seemed to understand him.

"You can see that we did not build right up against the buildings on either side. We created those cement walkways and benches." He pointed. "We built our structure thinner than we might have, so that occupants in the buildings on either side could still see out of their windows."

Ethan was enjoying this tremendously. He was so proud of what his father, Uncle Mel and Aunt Louise had produced. He loved to visit the Benton properties that his father had helped construct. They were all he had left of his dad. Steel, glass and concrete. But they were monuments that would endure for years to come.

They rode downtown to look at a low-rise housing development near the East River. Holly asked a million questions about why a door was placed where it was and what materials had been used for what.

Next was a refurbishment in Greenwich Village from the eighteen-nineties. "We spent a fortune on those windows!"

"They look original." Holly nodded in appreciation.

"That was the idea."

Then Ethan had Leonard park curbside in front of the massive Chelsea construction zone. The steel skeleton columns were up for all five buildings. Architectural renderings of what the finished project would look like were hung on fences and announced it to be "Benton Chelsea Plaza."

"This is all one property?" Holly was surprised by the size of the site.

"Five buildings of living, working and retail space. And I have commissioned a talented and, I might add, beautiful painter to do the artwork for the public spaces."

"The Chelsea project! This is it!"

Despite the cold, she lowered the car window and jutted out half of her torso to get a better view. Ethan bent forward to get an arm in front of her and pointed out some features.

Although he'd make sure Aunt Louise received the accolades, this venture was really all his. He'd made the difficult decisions and agonized over the setbacks. He knew this endeavor would have made Uncle Mel and his father proud if they had been alive to see it. And it would allow Aunt Louise to go into retirement on a high note.

His chest pressed into Holly's back as he pointed through the window. Impulse ordered him to move her scarf aside, so that he could kiss the back of her neck. Sheer will kept him from doing so. But it was being sorely tested in this close proximity.

It wasn't difficult to envision losing power over himself in an instant and laying her down on the car seat, climbing on top of her and delving into her softness. A softness he might not ever be able to return from.

Which was not at all part of their deal.

In fact, that kiss at dinner had been much too much. He himself had been startled by the force of it. He could sense it had unbalanced Holly as well.

He'd only meant to enhance their charade with some harmless and sanctioned affection. Prior to that his "guard and defend" strategy had helped him withstand her casual pats on his arm and his back all evening. Yet his own lips had barely touched hers when they'd begun to demand more, and he hadn't restrained himself in time. That kiss had been out of the scope of what was necessary in both intensity and duration.

His actions had overpowered him—a phenomenon he wasn't accustomed to. Lesson learned.

He forced himself back to describing the project. "For Building One we have leases for three fine dining restaurants and a food court of six casual establishments."

"So all that open space will be outdoor seating?"

"Exactly. And we will have a retractable awning with heating units for the colder months."

"I can imagine it."

He continued telling her about the plaza's features. As

with everything Benton Worldwide built, Ethan hoped to live up to architecture's fundamental principle of providing a building with both form and function for its users.

"I just thought of one other building I would like to take you to see. It is not a Benton property, but I think you will agree it has merit."

"You've brought me to the Empire State Building?" As she and Ethan got out of the car Holly craned her neck up at the monolith.

"As long as we were looking at New York architecture," he said, nodding, "I thought we ought to give this grand dame her due."

Taking her hand, Ethan led her into the Art Deco lobby, with its twenty-four-karat gold ceiling murals and marble walls. "Whew!" she whistled.

"Do you want to go up to the top?" he asked.

"Heck, *yes*."

But as they rode the escalator up one floor to the ticketing level memory slapped Holly hard.

She didn't mention to Ethan that she had been here once before. With Ricky. They'd come to New York for a long summer weekend. Stayed in a cheap hotel room in New Jersey.

The Empire State Building had been one of the sights Holly had most wanted to see on their trip. The weather had been hot and humid and the ticket lines crowded with tourists. Unlike tonight—late on a winter Wednesday.

Ricky had got impatient. He'd wanted a beer. He'd tugged her back down to street level, found a bar and that had been the last Holly had seen of the Empire State Building.

"Are you nervous about the elevator ride up?" Ethan asked, reacting to what must be showing on her face.

"No! I was just…um…let's go!"

Rocketing into the sky, Holly felt excitement pump through her veins. She was happy to leave old memories as far behind as she was leaving the asphalt of Thirty-Fourth Street and Fifth Avenue.

When they reached the top Ethan guided her quickly through the indoor viewpoints and exhibits to the outside observation deck.

And there it was.

Three hundred and sixty degrees of New York in the dazzling clear night.

It was utterly freezing. Two sorts of chills ran through her—one from the cold and the other sheer awe.

"Oh. My. Gosh." That was all she could say.

The city was so glorious, with the grid of its streets, the grandeur of its buildings and the galaxies of its lights.

They passed a few other visitors as they circled the deck. Holly gawked at Times Square. At Central Park. The Chrysler Building. The Statue of Liberty. The Hudson River.

She begged for a second lap around. "Let's take selfies!" She grinned as she pulled out her phone.

"You look very beautiful," Ethan said in a husky voice. "Your cheeks are pink from the cold."

She sensed him watching her more than he was looking at the views. He'd seen the sight of Manhattan before. It was probably all ho-hum to a global traveler like him. He had seen all the wonders of the world. And was probably amused at Holly's enthusiasm.

But he gamely put his arm around her and they posed to get photos with the skyline behind them, the Brooklyn Bridge in the distance. Holly surrendered the phone to him, to lift it higher than she could. He clicked several shots.

As he handed the phone back to her he kissed her on the cheek.

"I am *so* sorry." He backed away. "I did not mean to do that. I have no idea why I did."

"Maybe because a million romantic movie scenes have taken place right here?"

"Yes, that must be it. My apologies. It will not happen again."

She braved it and said what she wanted to say. "Actually, I'm glad you did. At dinner in front of your aunt and Fernando I got so flustered when you kissed me. I think I'll need to practice physical contact with you until it feels more expected."

She wasn't sure if she had really said that out loud or merely thought it. Rehearse kissing Ethan? That was insane.

"You might be right."

He moved in front of her so they were face to face. With her back to the observation deck's railing. The glistening city behind her.

Her breath sputtered. "In order to be convincing…"

Ethan arched down and brushed his mouth ever so slightly against hers. A wisp of his breath warmed her lips when he asked, "So, for example, you need to practice doing that?"

"Uh-huh," she squeaked out.

Why did he have to be so attractive? This would be much easier if she had become the fake fiancée of an unappealing man who didn't ignite her inside.

Clearly practice was all that was needed. Practice would make perfect. Eventually she'd become numb to him. Kissing would be a choreographed action they'd perform like trained seals.

She was sure of it.

"What about this?" he taunted, and more strength applied a firmer kiss to her lips.

A jolt shot up her back. Her hips rocked forward uncontrollably.

"I… I…" She struggled to take in a complete breath. "I think I need to work on that one."

She tilted her head back for mercy.

Giving her none, he took both sides of her face in his two hands and drew her to him. He kissed her yet again. Harder. Longer.

"Do we need to rehearse this?"

Now he'd opened his mouth. And he didn't stop there. The tip of his tongue parted her lips. Forced her tongue to meet his. Drove her to take. Give. Insist on more.

A dark moan rumbled from low in his gut.

A group of tourists strode past, ignoring them and pointing out landmarks in spirited voices. Holly couldn't see them. Ethan was all she could see.

His hands slid from the sides of her face slowly down her arms to the tips of her fingers. His lips traced across her jaw and then he murmured into her neck, "Do you think an engaged couple might need to kiss like that on occasion?"

"I do," she whispered.

He took hold of her hips and crushed himself into her. Pinned her back against the railing. She stretched her arms up around his neck, going pliant and yielding against the steel of his body.

With New York as her witness, he kissed her again and again and again. Until they had only one heartbeat. Until there could be no doubt in anyone's mind that this was a couple who were deeply in love.

CHAPTER EIGHT

FLOATING ON A CLOUD. Ethan had heard that saying before but this was the first time he'd experienced what it meant. Yes, his physical body lay on the uncomfortable leather sofa that was too small to stretch out on. But his heart and soul wafted above him in a silken, curvy vision he never wanted to wake from.

Of course, real sleep eluded him. It seemed an utter waste of time when Holly Motta was in the world. Sleep would just be hours and minutes spent away from thinking about her. What if, during sleep, his subconscious drifted away from the cocoon of her embrace? No, sleep was not time well spent. Not when instead he could linger in this half-daze, filled with the memory of her velvety lips on his and her long arms wrapped around him.

Though reality nagged at him.

After that mind-bending interlude of kissing at the Empire State Building they both knew that something unintentional, inappropriate and very dangerous had passed between them. Something they were going to need to backtrack from. To run from. And to return themselves to the "strictly business" contract they had made.

During the car ride afterward they'd chit-chatted about the architecture of a couple of noteworthy buildings along the way. Once they'd got home Holly hadn't been able to get away from him fast enough. She'd emerged from the bathroom in a tee shirt and pajama shorts, poured herself a glass of water, voiced a quick good-night and then rapped the bedroom door closed with her foot.

Ethan hoped that she was in his bed, resting in peaceful sleep. At least one of them ought to be. If he was being honest, he also hoped that she was having sweet dreams about him. Just as he was drifting in his trance about her.

As the endless night wore on Ethan's elation turned to irritation. This was not what he'd signed up for. Lying awake thinking about a woman? *No deal!*

He couldn't afford to have that kind of preoccupation in his life. None of his plans included a woman.

Sure, he could enjoy the company of the exotic and enticing females that his travels put him in contact with. That was a game he could play indefinitely. He wanted something from them that they'd readily give in exchange for a taste of his affluence and the limelight. Then they would want more and he would move on. He knew the routine well.

For all his aunt's prodding, Ethan hadn't ever truly acknowledged the possibility of really devoting himself to someone and building an inner circle with them. A private life together. Not after what he'd seen of the world. Not after his mother.

Blasted Holly! She'd exploded into his life and detonated every stronghold he held.

Worse still, to all intents and purposes he had reached the point of no return with her. He'd already introduced her to Aunt Louise. The gala was in three days. It would be a huge setback to back out now.

There was no choice but to see this through. However, once his aunt had stepped down and was securely ensconced in the warm Barbados sand, Ethan might have to cut the Holly engagement short. He couldn't take much more of this.

Uncle Mel had taught him that admitting and analyzing his mistakes was the crucial first step toward moving forward. Ethan had made a grave error in misjudging his own ability to keep this a purely business transaction.

Or perhaps it was just Holly. He'd chosen the wrong person for the job.

Holly was testimony that his aunt and uncle might be right—that an authentic love might be out there in the world for him. A love that was worth bowing to and sacrificing for. That defined his future and ordered everything else to work around it.

Which was not at all where Ethan was headed.

Argh! The road not taken… If only he had stuck to his original plan to hire an actress. She'd have been a consummate professional who knew exactly how to separate reality from performance. Her expertise would have shown him the way.

Just for torture, he flicked on a lamp and snatched his tablet from the coffee table. He clicked onto the website of the talent agency where he had located his original choice. The—unfortunately for him—pregnant Penelope Perkins. The website featured headshot photos of the talent they represented. Tap on the photo and a short bio appeared.

Ethan leaned back on the couch and studied Sienna Freeman. A willowy redhead with a daisy in her hair. An inquiring click told him that she had performed at regional theatres throughout the country, portraying the ingénue in famous American musicals. She looked as if she could have easily been groomed to play the fiancée in Ethan's little domestic drama. A sweet-faced young woman.

Trouble was, she wasn't Holly.

Gabrielle Rivera was a temptress with dark hair and crimson lips. A substantial list of her appearances in television comedies and commercials proved she was capable of working in a wide range of situations. Gabrielle would probably handle herself beautifully at important occasions. A fine choice.

Her fatal flaw? She wasn't Holly.

Glamazon Zara Reed was picture-perfect for a socialite wife. With her blond tresses swept into an up-do, Zara looked born to hang on a wealthy man's arm. Add in her master's degree in psychology and small roles in quirky films, and you had one convincing package. A jaw-dropper.

But—poor Zara. She simply wasn't Holly.

Enough! Ethan put the tablet down, turned off the light and attempted his now customary bent position on the sofa. Every molecule in his body screamed Holly's name.

He tossed until dawn, exhausted and annoyed.

Ethan came into the kitchen after he'd showered. Holly was picking at the apple crisp from the baking dish they had managed to stick in the refrigerator last night after Aunt Louise and Fernando had left.

Before they'd gone out looking at buildings. And at each other.

He joined her in scavenging through the mess of the kitchen for breakfast. "Is there coffee?"

She nodded. Once again, the cramped space was making her uneasy. Holly winced at every accidental slide against Ethan's starched white shirt or suit pants as she prepared two cups of java.

There had been quite enough touching him last night. She needed a break.

With him carrying the coffee, she followed him to the table with the apple crisp. She licked bits off her fingers as she folded herself into a chair.

"We could use forks," he suggested, "like evolved humans."

"Sorry if I'm not civilized enough for you."

"I did not say that."

He imitated her by gnawing his own fingerful of the leftover desert. Trying to make her laugh. Unsuccessfully.

Not that he didn't look cute doing it.

"I think it's obvious," she sneered.

Truth was, she was more than a little ticked off at what had happened last night at the Empire State Building. Even though she had asked for it. But how *dare* he kiss her like that if it didn't mean anything to him? That went way beyond the call of duty in this assignment she'd consented to.

Of course she'd had her part in it. She certainly hadn't pushed him away. The opposite, in fact. His kisses had fed a vital nutrient into her body that she had been starved of for so long she hadn't even known she was ravenous for it.

Nonetheless, she was still furious at him for stoking that hunger.

"What I think is obvious…" he paused for a sip of coffee "…is that you are angry at me and I do not know why."

"Welcome to marriage."

"No surprise I have steered clear of it."

She undid and redid her ponytail, buying a moment to regroup. Deciding to be honest.

"We went too far last night."

"I agree completely," he replied quickly.

"You do?"

His kisses hadn't offered any apology. They had been the kisses of a man entitled to his desires, who confidently took them with no cause for second guesses.

"Clearly we need to define the parameters of our physical contact," he stated, as if he was discussing an architectural floor plan. "It is important that we keep any sentiment out of the framework."

Was he admitting that he had felt as much as she had in that transcendental swirl of urgent kisses and intimate embraces? Or was he scolding her for crossing boundaries?

"It's my fault," she said, strategizing. "I asked you for some practice kissing because I don't want us to appear awkward in front of other people."

He took a minute to measure her words, carefully contemplating them before he responded.

"We simply got carried away," he concluded. "We will not do it again."

Inexplicably, her heart crashed to the floor. Which made no sense—because not passionately kissing Ethan Benton again was exactly what *did* need to happen.

"Right…" she granted. Yet sadness ricocheted between her ears.

As a diffuser, she munched on another chunk of the apple dessert.

Clearly no longer interested in the leftovers, Ethan reached for his phone. He ignored her to swipe, read and type.

She looked at her painting of him on the wall. She had never painted Ricky, nor the other couple of men she had dated. None of them had gotten under her skin like Ethan had. Filling her not only with the inclination but with the outright necessity to bring her brush to his likeness.

Ethan was like the multi-faceted diamond she wore on her finger. Every way she turned she saw something new. Something more. Something unexpected. Something unfathomable. She could paint him a hundred times and still not be done.

Eventually he glanced up and observed her, as if maybe he had forgotten she was in the room.

"So. Shall we establish some ground rules?"

"O-okay," she stumbled, unsure where he was going with this.

"I believe we *will* need to kiss on occasion. We will certainly want a convincing display of affection at the shareholders' gala, when our engagement is announced."

Holly braced herself, suddenly unsure if she was really going to be able to go through with this charade. She felt ill-suited to the task. It was too much.

"I think it will be beneficial for us to define what type of kissing is necessary," he continued.

"Absolutely," she bluffed, shifting in her seat.

"For example, I see no need for our tongues to touch, as they did last night."

Well, that was for sure. Her head and heart couldn't afford any more kisses like last night's. The kind that made a girl forget that she was only an employee of the most compelling and sexy man she had ever met. A man who had made it clear that he had hired her to help him protect his aunt, the only woman he'd ever love.

A fact she'd be wise to keep in the forefront of her mind.

Which his kisses completely clouded.

"Got it—no tongues." She nodded once and reached her hand across the table to shake his in a gentlemen's agreement.

Ethan's mouth hooked up as he shook her hand. He was amused by her gesture of sportsmanship.

Except he didn't let go of her hand after the shake. In fact he fought to keep it like a possession he'd battle to the ground for. He turned it over and caressed the tops of her fingers with the pad of his thumb.

"I'd prefer it if you didn't press your body into mine." Holly yanked her hand free and continued. She sparked at the memory of last night's six feet and three inches of solid manpower searing into her.

"How far away shall I stand?" he asked, holding his thumb and forefinger apart as a measurement. "This far?"

"Further than that."

Widening the gap between his fingers, he tilted his head. "This far?"

"At least."

"And would that be all of my body? Or just certain parts?"

Oh, Lordy, he was mocking her.

"Probably all parts." She kept going. "Of course we should have friendly hugs, but nothing prolonged."

"Shall I program a timer?" He smirked.

She lifted her palms in surrender. "Look, it was your idea to lay down some guidelines."

"You are right. I did not realize how ludicrous it would sound stated aloud." He abruptly stood and gathered his phone, tablet, keys and wallet. "For the moment we need not be concerned about our proximity to each other. My schedule today is filled with appointments."

With that, he turned toward the front door. Holly shifted her eyes to spy him putting on his suit jacket followed by his overcoat. He picked up a roll of architectural blueprints that had been propped up beside the door, and out he went.

Holly wasn't exactly sure why a sharp tear stung her cheek.

The left side needed more of the muddy purple she had mixed. Holly dipped thin bristles into the unusual color and applied them to her canvas. When they'd been at the art supply store Ethan had insisted on buying her a full range of brushes—a luxury she wasn't used to. She flicked tiny lines with a brush that was ideal for the task of depicting the rain outside.

Music blared from her phone—a pop singer belting on about how it was time to move on from a man who had done her wrong.

A wild sprawl of buildings and weather... Holly couldn't

decide whether or not she liked this painting. It didn't matter, though. The important thing was the *doing*.

Painting had always been Holly's best friend. It had kept her alive during a tumultuous childhood with an unstable mother and a man she'd called her father whom she had seen so few times she could count them on her fingers. Painting had got her through a disaster of a marriage to a selfish man-child. And then through an ugly divorce.

Painting was her escape. Her entertainment. Her coping mechanism. Her voice. Her salvation.

Early on, her brother, Vince, had found sports. And she'd discovered canvas and color. It was unimaginable where they'd be without those outlets.

In the past few years she had been fortunate enough to have been able to make some money creating artwork for paying clients. But in times of trouble she still picked up her brush purely for emotional release. For safety. For comfort.

Which was what was required now. Because she was disturbed and confused. Art gave her a little bit of a sanctuary in an unpredictable world.

So she had re-created her little studio area after packing it up for Louise and Fernando's visit last night. And she'd got back to work.

As often happened when she was painting, her problems became evident.

She had developed strong feelings for Ethan. And if that wasn't bad enough, she sensed the same might be happening for him.

How he managed to be so volatile while remaining so formal she'd never understand. He was in control of himself, yet there was a barely masked vulnerability there. Manners and restraint mixed with something brutal and pounding.

Those kisses atop the Empire State Building had come

from somewhere organic inside him. Beyond rational intent. That kind of intensity couldn't have been plotted.

In spite of that he would never care for her as anything more than an employee. Plain and simple. Even if he did, he would clamp his emotions down and lock them away as soon as he acknowledged them. He was too strong and too true ever to be swayed once he'd made a decision.

A means to an end. That was all she was to him.

And he to her.

Her phone buzzed.

"Ethan, here."

"Hi."

"I wanted to apologize for making light of your concerns about what physical interaction between us would be appropriate."

"I just don't want to mess up at the gala. I'm worried I'm going to get flustered, like I did at dinner last night. I want everything to go right for you and your plan for Aunt Louise."

"I agree that we could use more training sessions where we are surrounded by other people. I have a charity event to attend tonight. You and I will go together. As colleagues."

That was a terrific idea. She wanted to fulfill her end of the contract and make this arrangement work with Ethan. He was offering her the door into a New York that she could never open on her own. How hard could it be? He'd contracted her for a job that she was capable of doing. She just needed to keep the right mindset, purpose and goals.

An evening as colleagues. *Perfect*.

A couple of hours later the building's doorman knocked and handed Holly a delivery. She thanked him and carried the large white box to the table. Untying the gold ribbon that gave the box the appearance of a gift, she lifted the lid. A notecard was tucked on top of the gold tissue paper concealing the contents.

Tiny dress. Warm coat.
See you at the dock.
Ethan.

She unfolded the tissue to discover a black sequined party dress. It was sinfully short, with thin straps and a scooped back. Holly sucked in an audible whoosh of air. She couldn't believe that Ethan had sent her this sexy slip of a dress. Was this what his *colleagues* wore?

Tingles exploded all over her body.

For all the clothes he had already purchased for her, he must have thought none of them were just right for the charity event he was taking her to tonight.

Anticipation rocketed through her.

The warm coat—cream-colored, in a heavy wool—he had already bought her. The reference to a dock must mean they were going to be on or near a boat. The mystery of it felt hopelessly romantic, even though with Ethan she knew it wasn't. Nonetheless, she could hardly wait until nightfall.

Leonard picked her up at the scheduled time and transported her to the Battery Park dock where Ethan was waiting to open the car door. He extended his hand to help her out of the car. It was chilly, but there was no rain, and she wore her coat open over the new dress. Admittedly to show it off.

"Thank you, Leonard," Ethan called to his driver and closed the passenger door. To Holly he said, after a leisurely once-over, "I knew you would look stunning in that."

Their eyes met. She smiled. The left side of his mouth curved up.

"Shall we?" He offered his bent arm and she slipped hers through. But then he glanced down and stopped with caution. "Oh. Right." He lightly touched her engagement ring. "I generally do not bring a date to events like this.

Because our arrangement—rather, our engagement—will not be announced until the gala, would you mind terribly…?" His voice trailed out.

"No, of course not," she responded, hoping he didn't see the rush of disappointment sweep across her.

She slithered the diamond off her finger. She also hoped that, in the moonlight, he hadn't noticed that she'd been unable to remove every fleck of paint from her cuticles. She'd scrubbed her hands raw, but this was the best she could do. With any luck the stylists he'd hired to spruce her up for the gala would have some magic tricks up their sleeves.

"Shall I keep it?" he asked, and he took the ring from her and secured it in his pocket before she'd had a chance to answer. "I will introduce you as a coworker. We can have the evening to practice being comfortable with each other's company in public and nothing more."

"Exactly."

He presented his bent arm to her again. "All aboard."

As they ascended the gangway, Ethan waved politely to a few people, this way and that.

"Who was that?" Holly asked. "Where are we going?"

"Tonight is a fund-raiser for a private organization I belong to that supports maintenance of the Statue of Liberty as state funding is not sufficient. We will cruise to Liberty Island. The vantage point is spectacular. I think you will enjoy it."

The yacht set off into the New York Harbor, away from lower Manhattan. Champagne was passed on trays. Ethan and Holly mingled with a few guests onboard, sharing mainly superficial banter.

He introduced her as part of his interior design team and she shook a few hands. When they were out of anyone's earshot he instructed, "You can discuss the Chelsea Plaza project. Tell people you are currently analyzing the requirements. That you are handling the art, and much will depend on what materials the furnishings are made of."

During their next chat, around a standing cocktail table, the project came up. Holly interjected with, "We are assessing how people will move through the public spaces."

Ethan subtly nodded his approval. Holly was grateful for the positive reinforcement. She had never interacted with these mega-rich type of people before. Many of them were older than her—men in dark suits and women in their finest jewels. Wall Street leaders, heads of corporations, prominent doctors and lawyers. All of whom, apparently, with their charity dollars, were helping to keep the Statue of Liberty standing proud.

There would probably be many more people like this at the shareholders' gala on Saturday. Ethan had been smart to bring Holly here, so she could get a taste of this world she knew nothing about.

As they ferried closer to Liberty, Ethan led Holly to the yacht's railing to gain the best view.

"She is amazing."

Holly could only gawk up at the massive copper statue, famously green with its patina of age. From the spikes of Liberty's crown—which Ethan had told her represented rays of light—to the broken chain at her feet symbolizing freedom, she was a towering monument to emancipation. And her torch was a beacon of enlightenment.

Lady Liberty seemed to speak directly to Holly tonight. Holly looked into her eyes and pleaded for her wisdom and guidance.

"'Give me your tired, your poor...' Isn't that poem about this statue?" she asked Ethan.

"*The New Colossus* by Emma Lazarus."

"'Your huddled masses yearning to breathe free.'" Holly

had been suffocating in Florida. All her ghosts were there. "Maybe in New York *I* can breathe."

"What has constricted you?"

Making up for her mother's failings, with no father in the picture. Protecting her brother. Appeasing her explosive ex-husband.

"Where I come from nobody thinks big. Everyone is just trying to survive one more day."

Ethan moved a bit closer to Holly. They stood side by side while the yacht circled Liberty, allowing them to observe her from every angle.

"Fate has such irony. I know so many people who have everything," he said, "and yet it means nothing to them."

"Gratitude is its own gift."

He smiled wryly and nodded.

"As I mentioned, after Aunt Louise retires I plan to move Benton Worldwide's new construction solely into housing ventures for disadvantaged people. I like giving houses rather than just money. Because I can supply the knowledge and the labor to build them properly."

Colored lights began to flash on the deck and a band started playing in the dining room. Guests progressed to make their way inside the boat.

Ethan didn't move, and Holly stayed beside him as the boat turned and the tall buildings of Manhattan returned to their view.

"I have seen so much poverty in the world," Ethan continued musingly. "People living in shacks. In tents. In cardboard boxes. If I can help some of them have a safe and permanent home I will have accomplished something."

"You can only imagine what a house might mean to someone who doesn't have one." Holly knew about that first-hand, having moved from place to place so many times as a child.

"In any case..." Ethan shrugged "...for all my supposed

wealth and success, giving is the only thing that is truly satisfying."

Once all the other guests had filed inside, Ethan gestured for Holly to follow him in. At the dining tables they sat with some older couples who were discussing a landscaping project for the grounds around the statue.

When the band began a tamer version of a funky song that Holly loved, she stood and reached her hand down for Ethan's. "May I have this dance, sir?"

Ethan's signature smile made its slow journey from the left to the right side of his mouth. He stood and followed her onto the dance floor, where they joined some other couples.

She faced him and began to swing her hips back and forth to the music. When her hips jutted left, her head tipped right. Then she flung her head left and he hips responded to the right. Like ocean waves, her body became one undulating flow. Back and forth. Back and forth.

The dress was slinky against her skin. She loved how it swung a little with every move she made. From what she could surmise in Ethan's watchful eyes, he liked the movement of the dress, too.

At first he just rotated one shoulder forward and then the other, in a tentative sashay. But after a bit any self-consciousness dissolved and he let his body gyrate freely to the beat of the music.

He had a natural rhythm—just as Holly had known he would. It was part of that primitive side of him—the part he kept hidden away. The part she wished she could access.

Their eyes locked and their movements synchronized until they were undeniably dancing together.

There was no doubt of their attraction to each other. But they were doing a very good job of keeping the evening friendly and nothing more, just as planned.

As a matter of fact, when he had been talking on the

deck earlier, about the good feeling of giving, it had been as if Holly was an old pal he could confide in. Pals were good.

Which was why when the band switched to a slow song Holly turned to leave the dance floor. Slow dances weren't for buddies.

But a strong arm circled her waist.

"This doesn't fit in with our no touching policy this evening." Holly shook her head in resistance.

Ethan pulled her toward him and into a firm clinch. He secured her against him with a wide palm on her back.

Her breath hiccupped. Tonight was supposed to be time off from physical contact with him. After their intimacy at the Empire State Building last night had gone far outside the realm of their contract. Tonight, the last thing Holly needed was to have her face pressed against his neck, with the smell of his skin and his laundered shirt intoxicating her into a dangerous swoon.

"We may as well have a run-through, future Mrs. Benton," he murmured into her ear. "We will be expected to dance together at the gala."

He lifted one of her arms and placed her hand on his broad shoulder. He clasped her other hand in his.

"I don't know if I can do it," Holly protested.

"Surely I am not *that* irresistible."

She laughed, although that was only half funny. "What I meant was, I don't know how to partner-dance."

"Well, young lady, you are in luck. I happen to be three-time champion of the Oxford Ballroom Dance Society."

"Really?"

"No. Of course not."

He began moving and she followed in line.

"But it is not that difficult. Can you feel my thigh leading yours…?"

* * *

When they got home, before they retreated to their separate sleeping quarters, Ethan retrieved the engagement ring from his jacket pocket.

As he replaced it on her finger, he asked, "Holly, would you marry me…again?"

CHAPTER NINE

"WHO ON EARTH would notice the difference between a napkin color called Eggshell and another called Champagne?" Ethan bellowed to Holly as she made her way across the vast hotel ballroom. "And good morning."

"There's actually a big distinction." Holly jumped right in and snatched the two samples from him. She held one up in each hand to catch some of the room's light. "See— the Champagne is iridescent. The Eggshell is matte. It's a very different effect."

"Thank you for being here."

About an hour ago Ethan had called Holly and asked her to meet him here to finalize the details for tomorrow's gala. Aunt Louise was not feeling well.

"I would call in my assistant, Nathan, but I have him on a dozen other tasks right now."

Ethan's brow furrowed as he remembered yet more specifications he needed to take care of.

"What's wrong with Louise?" Holly inquired.

"She said she felt a bit weak and lightheaded."

"Will she be okay by tomorrow?"

"I hope so. She will stay upstairs today, resting in one of the suites we booked for the week. Fernando is with her. Not that *he* is of any help."

"What do you think triggered it?"

"Rainy weather is especially difficult for her. And, even though she likes to be involved in planning these galas, I think the strain is too much."

He'd feel immense relief once his aunt had retired and no longer bore the weight of continuing as CEO of their billion-dollar company. With any luck she'd be flying in from Barbados for next year's gala, with no cares other than what dress she should wear.

"I'm here to help, Ethan. What can I do?"

Holly's concern softened his tension. He gestured to the table in front of him—the only one in the bare ballroom with a tablecloth on it. Several place settings were laid out for approval, each complete with different options for china, napkins, silver and stemware. There were modern styles, and those that were more ornate. Some in classic shapes, others unusual.

"Can you make these decorative decisions? You are the artist," he said, and added with a whisper, "and the fiancée."

There was no one directly in earshot, but hotel employees bustled about doing their work. With camera phones and social media these days, Ethan wanted to be sure details of his engagement weren't released to the world any earlier than he wanted them to be.

"Oh. Good grief."

"What?"

He pointed to her hand. "The ring again. I am so sorry."

She gamely glided it off her finger, handed it to him and filled her cheeks with air to make a funny face.

"It is ludicrous. I apologize again. Now, Aunt Louise had started to select a certain color palette. She picked out this tablecloth…"

Holly lifted a corner of the linen draping the table and found an identifying label underneath. "This color is called Stone. I like its earthiness. Instead of choosing a lighter napkin, how about a darker one? Can we see samples that might be called something like Pewter or Slate?"

"Sweetheart, you can see anything you want as long as you get this taken care of."

He immediately regretted the endearment. It had fallen from his mouth spontaneously. He supposed that was what he'd need to be doing once they were announced as an engaged couple, so he might as well get used to it. Still, he wasn't in the habit of referring to women by pet names. Holly's widened eyes told him she was surprised by it as well.

Thankfully, one of the hotel's event managers was passing by. Ethan flagged down Priya to come talk to Holly. And to get him out of the moment.

As the two women conferred he stepped away to return a couple of missed phone calls. Which was a bit difficult because the napkins weren't the only things that reflected light from the ballroom's massive chandeliers.

Holly's lustrous hair, flowing freely long past her shoulders, framed her face with a glowing halo. Her sincere smile came easily during her conversation. Sidetracking him from his call to the point when he had to ask his site supervisor on the Bronx project to repeat what he had just said. Which was both embarrassing and unacceptable.

How many reminders did Ethan need that a woman had no place in his life?

She bounded over to him after her consultation with the event manager.

"I hope you don't mind, but I've had a vision. I did go with a pewter napkin. And a minimalist kind of china and flatware..." She rattled off details at a mile a minute. "With a silver napkin ring to give it a sort of elemental look. Earth and metal, kind of thing."

He mashed his lips to suppress a smile, although he was charmed at her zeal.

"And, if it's okay," she persisted, "I thought we could do a sleek centerpiece with white flowers in clear glass vases, to bring in a water element as well. I think it'll all tie together with the lighting." She pointed up to the modern chandeliers with their narrow pieces of glass. "Do you think your aunt would like that?"

"She will appreciate your creativity," he said after Holly's debriefing. "Miss Motta, it sounds like you have a knack for this sort of thing."

She shrugged. "I guess it's just a painter's eye. And at my own wed—"

Ethan's phone rang. He lifted one finger to signal to Holly to hold that thought while he took the call. "Yes, Nathan?"

Holly's cheeks turned pink. She bit her lip.

Something he wouldn't mind doing.

Sweetheart. He'd accidentally called her *sweetheart*.

"Schedule me for a late lunch with him next Tuesday at that restaurant he likes on Jane Street. Thank you." He turned his attention back to Holly, "Sorry—what were you saying?"

"Oh. Um… Just that Priya says the tech crew are here if you're ready to go to the podium."

"Come with me."

He took her hand. After taking the few stairs from the ballroom floor up to the stage, Ethan and Holly turned to face the empty event space. Tomorrow night Benton Worldwide Properties would once again fête many of their shareholders with an evening of appreciation. Close to a thousand people—some from nearby, others who had traveled far—would fill this grand room for the annual event.

Holly whistled. "What a breathtaking location for a dinner." She pointed to the large gold wall sculptures that circled the back of the room. "Those give the idea of waves in an ocean, don't they?"

Ethan surveyed the familiar surroundings. "The burgundy carpeting is new this year. It used to be a lighter color. That is about the only change I have noticed."

"You hold the dinner here every year?"

"We have been using this room for as long as I can remember. These galas are as ingrained into my family as birthdays and Christmas are to others."

This year's event wouldn't be a run-of-the-mill evening, though, when his and Holly's engagement was to be announced.

Holly gestured with her head toward the podium on the stage. "Will you be giving a speech?"

"The baton will pass to me next year," he said. Uncle Mel had always given the speech and, after he died Aunt Louise had taken over the duty. "Only a few of us know that this is the last time Aunt Louise will deliver the CEO's report."

Louise's retirement wouldn't be revealed at the gala. Ethan and his aunt had decided that the first step in her exit strategy would be to introduce his fiancée. That would cause enough pandemonium for one evening.

Shareholders could be tricky. They didn't like too many changes all at once. Benton Worldwide had already made them a lot of money by sticking to the original principles Uncle Melvin and Ethan's father had established when they'd started the company with one small apartment building in roughneck South Boston.

So only the engagement announcement would come at the gala. In a month, they'd inform the shareholders in writing that Louise Benton was retiring after a distinguished career. A month after that they'd throw a splashy retirement party.

Tomorrow night would belong to him and Holly Motta. In addition to their proclamation to the shareholders, a press release would notify the world that Ethan Benton had finally chosen a bride. Photos of them would appear in the business sections of newspapers and websites across the planet.

Ethan peered at Holly by his side on the stage. Sudden terror gripped him. What if this masquerade was too risky? This pretty young woman appeared to be genuine and of good will. But what if she wasn't? What if she was like every other woman he'd ever met? Deceptive. Manipulative. Out for herself.

He'd only met her a few days ago, for heaven's sake. It wasn't long enough to put her intentions to the test. And he still didn't know much about her other than what she'd chosen to disclose. Hopefully his head of security, Chip Foley, would get back to him soon with any information he had found. If there was something he didn't want exposed he'd need to figure out how to bury it so that the press didn't have a field-day.

Doubt coursed through him. What if Holly simply wasn't as capable a performer as he'd hired her to be? Maybe she'd crack under the spotlight and the attention. Confess that this was all a set-up, causing Benton Worldwide embarrassment and loss of credibility.

His mind whirled. What had he been thinking? In his haste to plan Aunt Louise's departure from public life before her medical condition diminished her position of respect, Ethan had made an uncharacteristically rash decision. If it was the wrong one his family would pay dearly for it for the rest of their lives.

However, there was no choice now but to take a leap of faith.

"Are you ready for this?" He took Holly's hand, as he would tomorrow. Her fingers were supple and comforting, and immediately slowed his breath.

"I may faint afterward, but I promise to put on a show," she answered amiably, lacing her fingers in his.

"Imagine every table filled with people in tuxedos and evening gowns. Staring at you."

Her shoulders lifted in a chuckle. "Gee, no pressure there!"

Her humor reassured him that she could pull this off. She wouldn't have agreed to it if she didn't know in her heart that she could handle it. And she'd done fine on the yacht last night.

Aunt Louise wanted this one thing for Ethan before she stepped away and let him officially run the company. He was determined to give it to her.

An astute woman, his aunt knew that Ethan's constant travel was to avoid settling down. He didn't have any sustained commitments outside of work. Hardly had a base other than his rarely visited corporate flat near their headquarters in Boston. He dated women—and then he didn't. He spent months alone on a boat. Socialized, then disappeared into a foreign country. He was free. There was nothing to tie him down. He could do whatever he wanted, go wherever he pleased. And he did.

His aunt believed that a fulfilled life took place on terra firma. She wanted him to find a home. A home that would shelter him from the topsy-turvy world of highs and lows, change and disappointment.

Home wasn't a place.

Home was love.

An all-encompassing love that he could count on. That could count on him. That made life worth living day after day. Year after year.

Because of Holly, Ethan had now had a glimpse into what it might be like to coexist with someone. Like he had last night on the Liberty cruise, easily sharing his thoughts and plans and hopes.

But he would stay firm in his resolve to go it alone.

And that was that.

That was his fate.

That was his destiny.

So he'd give Holly to his aunt as a retirement gift. Deliver her on a silver platter. Let the one woman who had ever been good to him hold the belief she most wanted.

But Ethan would not forget the truth.

"Mr. Benton?" A voice boomed from a dark corner of the ballroom. "We'd like to do a sound-check from the podium, if you wouldn't mind."

"Of course," Ethan said to the unseen technician.

Still clutching Holly's hand, he led her to the side of the stage before they parted. His fingers were reluctant to let go. Yet he dutifully took his place at the lectern and adjusted the microphone. Substituting for Aunt Louise, who would be introduced tomorrow to deliver her speech.

"Thank you for joining us this evening at Benton Worldwide Properties' annual shareholders' gala. We are so delighted you are here... Test, test. Test. Testing..."

Ethan dummied through as the technician made adjustments to the sound system.

"Without our shareholders we would not have experienced the global development... Hello, hello. You give us the inspiration... Thank you, thank you. Testing one, two, three."

He turned to wink at Holly. She grinned in response.

"Thank you, Mr. Benton," the technician called out. "Now we'd like to run the video, if you'd like to watch and okay?"

"Will do."

Ethan escorted Holly back down the steps to one of the tables. They took their seats as a screen was lowered from above the stage.

"Hey, do we get to sample the food?" Holly asked. "Quality control?"

"No, that is one department Fernando *is* actually handling. He was here earlier, approving everything with the chefs, before he went to attend to Aunt Louise."

"Rats!" She snapped her fingers, cute as could be.

Which made him want to kiss her.

Which was more irrational thinking he'd need to get a handle on.

Kissing was only for show, when people were watching. No more recreational kissing. The Empire State Building kissing shouldn't have happened. Where he'd thought he might have been able to keep kissing Holly until the end of the world.

His body quirked even now, remembering.

He locked his attention on the screen as the presentation began with a graphic of the company logo and some sprightly music. A slick narrator's voice explained a montage of all the Benton Worldwide projects that had been started or completed during the past year.

In another montage employees were shown holding babies, celebrating their children's college graduations, tossing a football at company picnics.

A historical section flashed older photos—one of Uncle Mel and Ethan's father, Joseph, holding shovels at a groundbreaking ceremony.

"That is my dad." Ethan pointed. His heart pinged as the image quickly gave way to the next photo. Joseph had died when he was nine. Twenty-five years ago. "I do not remember much about him anymore," he admitted.

Holly put a hand on his shoulder. He prickled, but didn't pull away despite his automatic itch to do so.

"Tell me one thing you do remember about him."

"That photo shows him in a suit. I can only think of him in a casual work shirt. Uncle Mel was the businessman. My father was always at the construction sites."

One glimpse of memory Ethan did have of his father was of when he'd come home from work at night. He'd greet Ethan and then head straight to the shower to wash off his honest day's work.

His mother was not a part of that picture. She would sequester herself in her private bedroom before Ethan came home from school, and there she'd stay throughout the evening. It had been a nanny who'd tended to Ethan in the afternoon.

Another older photo had clients at a job site, with Joseph in a hard hat on one side of them and Uncle Mel and Aunt Louise on the other side.

"Do you have any pictures that include your mother?"

"Oh, she was in that shot. We had her edited out. We cut her out of every photo."

Holly tilted her head, not understanding. "Why?"

Now he shook Holly's hand off his shoulder. He couldn't take her touch.

"Because we did not want her in any way associated with Benton Worldwide."

"But *why*?"

"My father and Uncle Mel worked hard for every dollar they made. They earned it. They deserved it. And they were loyal to the people who were loyal to them. Values my mother cared nothing for."

Ethan's blood pressure rose, notifying him to end this conversation. When Holly started to ask another question, his glare shut her down.

Another photo documented him and Aunt Louise in front of a gleaming high-rise building. "Ah, the Peachwood Center in Atlanta. One of my favorites."

The last photo had Aunt Louise surrounded by ten or so Benton executives in front of their headquarters. Even though in reality Ethan had been running the company since Aunt Louise's health had begun to fail, he still made sure that she got all the credit and glory.

"Is everything correct on the video, Mr. Benton?" the technician called from the back of the ballroom.

"Yes—thank you."

"May I trouble you for one more thing, sir? Can I get an okay for sound and lighting on the dance floor?"

Ethan stood and made his way to the polished wooden floor in the center of the ballroom. Fully surrounded by the burgundy carpet and the tables defining the perimeter, the dance floor was its own little world, and it was lit as such with a yellow tint and spotlights beaming down from the ceiling.

"Mr. Benton, we'd like to check the lighting with some movement. Would you be able to find someone to do a quick waltz around the dance floor for me?"

Naturally Ethan gestured to Holly. Stretching out his arm, he beckoned. "So, we dance again."

Holly stood and navigated between the tables in the empty ballroom to reach Ethan on the dance floor. She envisioned what he had described—how tomorrow night the room would be filled with well-dressed shareholders gaping at her. Not giving in to panic, she reminded herself that she was here to do a job. To supply what she'd offered.

A love ballad suitable for ballroom dancing began from the sound system. Ethan started to dance and Holly's body fell in line with his.

He'd taught her well last night, and although she didn't think she could pull off any fancy ballroom dance moves she didn't trip all over his feet.

The lights were so bright on the dance floor that she could hardly see out to the tables. Which didn't matter that much because she really only wanted to close her eyes and enjoy the moment. The croon of the singer… Ethan's sure steps… His rock-sturdy chest…

Dancing with him, she thought they really were a couple—an entity that was larger than the sum of two individuals.

Ah... Her head fit so well underneath his chin as they danced. Being tall, she'd always had a sense of herself as being gawky around Ricky and the other men she had dated. She loved being encompassed by Ethan's height and width. As they glided across the dance floor, she felt graceful. A fairy princess. A prom queen. The object of attention.

All things she wasn't.

How would it be tomorrow, with a roomful of guests scrutinizing her? They wouldn't think she was beautiful enough for a man like Ethan! Everyone would know that she wasn't pedigreed and educated. They'd wonder why a Benton had settled for someone as ordinary as her.

Although she would be wearing the magnificent sky-blue gown covered in crystals. That gown alone would convince leaders and kings that she was one of them. Her hair and makeup would be professionally done. The smoke and mirrors tricks would be believable.

She'd hobnobbed with the New York elite last night and no one had guessed that she was not of their social standing. They hadn't known that she'd grown up in a trailer park with an unmarried mother who'd been too drunk to get out of bed half of the time.

Of course at the gala Ethan's fiancée would be under closer examination.

She tilted her head back to study her hand on Ethan's shoulder. Just as she had last night, she actually missed wearing the gargantuan diamond ring that labeled her Ethan's intended. She thought back to the paper ring he had used to propose to her. When he had bent down on one knee with a ring made from a beer bottle label.

And then she flashed back to the shopping spree on Fifth Avenue. To the blue topaz ring she had loved. But

Ethan was right, of course. The ring he'd chosen was one befitting the future Mrs. Benton.

Leaning back further, to look up into Ethan's handsome face, she asked him, "Being in the spotlight doesn't faze you in the least?"

"I suppose I have always been visible to the shareholders. They watched me grow up."

"You came to the galas as a child?"

His muscles twitched. "When I was younger I was kept upstairs in a suite with my mother, who hated these evenings. We would come down and make an appearance."

Holly had noticed that Ethan's voice became squeezed every time his mother came up in conversation. Hints of rage had come spitting out when he'd explained how they had edited her out of all the photos in the slideshow.

"Wasn't your mother obligated to attend?" Holly persisted.

"She would call the kitchen to find out exactly what time dinner was being served. A half-hour before she would trot me down here in a tuxedo. We would do our annual mother-and-son spin around this dance floor. Then she would tug me to the exit, offering excuses that it was my bedtime or that she had a migraine."

"What about your dad?"

"He was not much the tuxedo-and-martini type, but he would soldier through alone. My mother was not gracious, like Aunt Louise. She would not mingle and exchange pleasantries with the guests. Not even to support my father. He knew that she was not an asset to the company."

"Was it awful for you, being paraded around?"

"Not really. I understood at an early age that my mother was not good for business but that I was. Whether it had been a profitable year or a struggle, seeing that there was a next generation of leadership instilled confidence in the shareholders. I have always been proud to represent our company."

"Is your mother still alive?"

"I have no idea," he bit out. "Nor do I care in the least. I have always assumed the shareholders believe that she went into seclusion and retired from public life after my father died."

With that, he tightened his hold around Holly's waist, bolted her against him and guided her with an absolute command that started at the top of his head and ended at the tip of his toes.

Holly molded herself to him and allowed his confident lead. Knowing that talk of his mother had unleashed the beast that he had now locked back into the cage inside him.

As they circled the music got louder, then softer. The low bass tones became more pronounced and then were corrected. Lights were adjusted as well, becoming hotter, then diffused and milky.

"Just one minute more, Mr. Benton!" the technician announced.

The music changed to a swinging standard.

Ethan relaxed his grip and backed Holly away to arm's distance ready for a quickstep. He twirled her once under his arm. She stumbled and they chuckled into each other's eyes.

His head tilted to the side. They leaned in toward each other's smiles. Drawn to each other.

Out of the corner of her eye Holly saw Aunt Louise's husband, Fernando, enter the ballroom and scurry toward them.

When they had come to the apartment for dinner she had noticed the way Fernando walked with small, mincing steps. She hadn't liked how he had snooped at the things on Ethan's desk and taken a fax from the machine. And she had overheard him telling Ethan that he didn't want to spend his life in Barbados when Louise retired.

But at this moment it was important for them to unify for the sake of Louise. Since the older woman wasn't well today, Ethan and Fernando had taken charge of the final details for the gala. Ethan had to be grateful for whatever help Fernando was offering. Perhaps he had a report on the status of the menu...

"I've been trying to call you!" Fernando approached and yapped at Ethan.

Ethan glanced over to one of the empty tables, where he had left his phone while he was on stage at the podium and while he and Holly had danced. "Is everything in order?" he asked.

"No, it's not. Louise has taken a bad fall. I've called the paramedics."

CHAPTER TEN

ETHAN LED THE charge out of the ballroom and toward the hotel elevators, with Fernando and Holly racing behind him to keep up. When they reached the bronze elevator bank Ethan rapped the call button incessantly until one set of doors opened. Pressing for the twenty-sixth floor as soon as he'd stepped in, he backed against the gilded and mirrored wall of the elevator car.

His neck muscles pulsed. As the elevator ascended he kept his eyes peeled on the digital read-out of the floor numbers.

One, two, seven, twelve...

"What happened?" He forced the question out of a tight throat.

"Louise had been resting on the sofa in the suite's living room," Fernando reported. "She stood up and said she was going to make a phone call. Then, as she started to walk, she tripped on the coffee table and fell face-forward."

"Why did you not help her get up from the sofa in the first place?" Ethan seethed.

"She didn't tell me she was going to stand up. She just did it. I rushed to her, but it was too late."

Ethan's jaw ground as he fought to keep himself together. This incompetent idiot should have never been allowed to care for Aunt Louise. She was going to need full-time nurses. He'd arrange that immediately.

The read-out reached twenty-three, twenty-four…

On the twenty-sixth floor, Ethan pushed through the elevator doors before they had fully opened. Holly and Fernando followed. At the room's door, he snatched the key card from Fernando's hand.

Ethan rushed into the suite. "Aunt Louise?"

Louise sat on the floor with her back against the sofa. Angry scrapes had left red stripes across her right cheek and her knees. She massaged her wrist.

"I'm all right, dear," she assured him in a fairly steady voice. "Don't embarrass me any more than I've already embarrassed myself."

"There is no reason to be embarrassed," Ethan said, trying to soothe her. These incidences must be so humiliating for her. She'd always been such an able woman.

"Falls happen," Fernando chimed in. "We've been here before, Louise. You'll be fine."

Ethan fired a piercing glower at Fernando. He didn't need to try to make light of the situation.

"Oh, goodness. Holly!" Louise spotted Holly standing back from them. She managed a dry smile. "Somehow I've become an old woman."

"Thank goodness you weren't hurt worse." Holly nodded her respect.

"At this point we do not know if or how much she is injured," Ethan snapped, angry with everyone. "She needs to be examined."

Right on cue, there was a soft knock on the door. Ethan let in the hotel manager, who confirmed that they were expecting paramedics. Two emergency medical technicians filed in.

One checked Louise's vital signs, such as her blood pressure and heart-rate. He shone a small light into her eyes. Another technician asked questions about her medical history and what had happened.

While that was going on Ethan noticed Fernando pouring himself a cocktail. Holly had noticed too.

He and Holly raised eyebrows at each other. This was hardly a time for drinks.

Ethan clenched his fists and mashed his lips tightly. He stood silently.

Fernando had accused Ethan at dinner the other night of finding himself a wife just so that Louise would retire. Fernando had said he had no intention of spending his life on boring Barbados, as he characterized it, with Louise.

So, following that logic, Fernando should be doing everything he could to try to keep Louise as healthy as possible. Yet he obviously didn't bother with trivial matters, such as protecting her from falling. And now—with paramedics in the room, no less—he clearly thought it was cocktail hour.

"There don't appear to be any broken bones," one of the technicians informed them. "But, given her overall medical condition, we're going to transport her to the hospital for a more complete evaluation."

Ethan brought a hand over his mouth, overcome with worry. This woman had shown him so much love—had gone above and beyond the call of duty for him his entire life. Maybe his caring so much for his aunt was a sign. That he was capable of loyalty. Of devotion.

He refused his inclination to look over to Holly.

The technician issued instructions into his phone.

Fernando walked over to pat Louise gently on the shoulder in between sips of his drink.

"Can we take her down in a private elevator?" Ethan asked the manager, who waited quietly beside the door. "And out through a private garage? Many of our shareholders are staying here at the hotel, and we would like to keep this matter to ourselves."

"Of course, Mr. Benton."

Fernando settled himself closer to where Ethan was standing. "Clever..." he said under his breath. "Always thinking about image. I've got a little surprise for you with regards to that."

Ethan whipped his head to look into Fernando's eyes. "What on earth are you talking about at a time like this?" he demanded.

Two more paramedics came through the door with a stretcher.

Louise protested, "Oh, please, gentlemen—a wheel-chair would do."

"It's for your protection, ma'am."

"I will ride in the ambulance with Louise," Ethan declared.

"No. *I* will," Fernando countered.

"Family only, please," one of the technicians said over his shoulder as he secured Louise onto the stretcher.

"I'm her husband."

"I am coming as well," Ethan insisted.

To the outside eye they must look like an odd sort of family. Elderly Aunt Louise. Nephew Ethan, who was probably being mistaken for her son, and Holly for his wife. Then Fernando, with his tanning salon skin and over-styled hair, who looked exactly the part of a cougar's hus-band.

The hotel manager headed the pack as the technicians began wheeling the stretcher out of the suite. Fernando and Ethan followed closely behind.

Ethan turned his head back to Holly. "You go home to the apartment."

"I'd like to come to the hospital, too."

Irritated at even having to discuss this further, Ethan

repeated his order. "There is no need for you to be at the hospital. Go back to the apartment."

The hotel manager led them to a private elevator and swiped her access card.

Ethan dashed a text into his phone.

"I could take a taxi and meet you there," Holly pleaded. "I want to be there for you and—"

He cut her off. "I have just instructed Leonard to pick you up in front of the hotel."

This was a private matter that Holly had no place in, despite appearances. While he had certainly become accustomed to having her around, she was still only an employee, and Louise's health was a personal thing. Ethan did not want Holly to overhear any discussions with doctors, or any information regarding a prognosis for his aunt. What Holly had just witnessed in the suite was beyond what his fiancée-for-hire should be privy to.

Ethan feared that he was starting to lose his better judgment around Holly. It was becoming so easy, so natural to let her into his life. If he allowed himself to, he might long for her support at the hospital. He knew it would be hours of waiting and worrying while Aunt Louise was examined.

He had nothing to say to Fernando. Wouldn't sitting with Holly in the waiting area, sharing a paper cup full of coffee, huddled together, be a comfort?

No! Once again, he reminded himself of Holly's place in this dynamic. Despite how they might appear, to the paramedics or anyone else, Holly was not part of this family.

Not. Family.

He pointed down the hall toward the public elevator they had ridden up to the suite. "Holly, please return to ground floor and retrieve my things from the ballroom. Thank you."

Louise was wheeled into the private elevator, and everyone but Holly got in.

Just as the doors were closing Ethan saw in Holly's eyes that he'd upset her by not allowing her to come along. But this was no time to focus on her. She should know and respect that.

"I will phone you as soon as I hear anything, all right?"

He didn't wait for an answer.

So much for being part of the family.

Holly made it through the car ride home from the hotel, and it wasn't until she opened the door to the dark, empty apartment that tears spilled down her face.

Louise's condition was heartbreaking, and Holly hoped that she wasn't seriously injured after the tumble she'd taken. That she would be able to make it to the gala to-morrow night.

Ethan and Louise had such a finely tuned strategy to keep the extent of her illness hidden from the public. Holly admired their efforts. And thankfully the paramedics were only taking Louise to the hospital as a precaution.

She flipped on the lights. Slung her jacket on the coat rack. Kicked off her boots. And then she allowed in some self-pity. If she ever needed a reminder that this engagement was all a front, she had her proof. She was not, and nor would she ever be, a member of this clan.

Once they'd arrived at Louise's hotel suite Ethan had barely acknowledged her presence. Not that she would have expected him to pay lots of attention to her, but she had to admit she was surprised at how completely he had shut her out.

Holly had offered to go along to the hospital to be there for Louise *and* for Ethan—as a friend who rallied round when maybe a hand to hold would be welcome. But Ethan would have none of it, and hadn't been able to get her out of the picture swiftly enough.

Everything had moved so fast this week. How had she

got here? To feeling sorry for herself because she was left behind? How had she come to care so much for these people so quickly? She'd become so involved in Ethan's life she could hardly remember a time when she hadn't been. Had she forgotten who she was?

Holly Motta was an artist who had spent four long years married to the wrong man.

Ricky hadn't made it easy for her to leave. Even after she'd moved out of the last place they'd been living he'd shown up at her work and insisted on talking to her. Or he'd followed her car and confronted her at a supermarket or in a bank parking lot. It had got to the point that she'd had to change her phone number. Month after month he had refused to sign the legal documents divorcing them, leaving her hanging in limbo. Finally he'd given up and cut her loose.

It had taken her two years to feel truly unshackled from the demanding and possessive hold Ricky had on her. Now she was determined to move forward with her life. This prospect with Ethan had presented itself and she'd snatched it. The job, this apartment, the clothes...the promise of a glamorous escapade with an exciting man.

Nothing wrong with any of that. Life was throwing her a bone, for once. And she was taking it. Life on life's terms.

The problem was the illusion was so convincing that she was starting to buy it.

Twenty-nine years of hurt overtook her. She wasn't tough, like New York. She couldn't endure another defeat. Withstand another wound. Her heart functioned in broken pieces that were only taped together and could collapse at any minute. Maybe this masquerade was too dangerous. She didn't think she had it in her to bounce back from anguish yet again.

Restless, she went to the kitchen. Drank a full glass of water in one gulp. It had been hours since she'd eaten. A few slices of cheese and bread went down easily as she munched them standing up.

She hoped Ethan would get a bite to eat at the hospital. He'd be hungry, too. *Ugh!* She needed to stop caring about things like whether or not he had eaten. Had to break her habit of always looking after people.

She paced back to the living room. Judged the paintings she had been working on in the little studio area she had created by the window. They were a good start to the ideas she had in her head. A drawing pad perched on the easel. She mindlessly picked up a stick of charcoal and began to put it to paper.

After a few minutes she cranked up some funky music and swung her hips from left to right to the beat. A little sketching, a little boogie-woogie—that was always how she got through everything in her life.

Curved lines on the page. A man's jaw. Not square and chiseled like Ethan's. That buzz-cut hair. The thick swash of eyelashes.

A smile crossed her lips.

Small ears. The rounded shoulders. The only person she could count on. Her brother.

Yet she hadn't been honest with Vince about the events of the past few days. She had called him the first night she was here, when the mix-up with the apartment had started everything that had come since. She'd hinted that something had come her way. Vince had reminded her that it was *her* time now. That she should take hold of any prospect life threw at her.

They'd had so little in the way of support as kids. They'd always had to be each other's cheering section.

Straight up or fall down... Holly mouthed their childhood chant.

They had been texting every day, as they always did. She'd told him that New York was amazing. That it was mostly raining. But she hadn't told him about this weird arrangement she'd agreed to. Which had become a wild rollercoaster of feeling so right and then, in the next moment, feeling so wrong.

She hadn't even told Vince about meeting Ethan. And she hadn't told Ethan about her rat ex-husband, Ricky. It wasn't like her to keep secrets. But she didn't know where anything stood anymore. She didn't want to make things more complicated than they already were. Even if nothing were to work out for her here in New York, Holly needed to make sure that Ethan kept his word about helping Vince.

Her brother was a good man. She was so proud of him. Every day she hoped and prayed for a bright future for him. That separately, yet bound in spirit, they'd rise up like phoenixes from the ashes of their childhood.

She thumbed her phone.

"Holz?" Vince used his nickname for his sister.

"Vinz!" Holly sandwiched the phone between her ear and her shoulder as she finished drawing her brother's arm. Their builds were so different... It was only in the eyes of their mother where the resemblance was undeniable.

"How's New York treating you?"

"Oh... I kinda got involved in something I thought was one thing but now it seems like it's another."

As in tonight. Which had been reinforcement of the fact that Ethan would never regard her as anything more than a hired hand. That the feelings she'd started to have for him could only lead to misfortune.

"What are you talking about?"

"I don't know... I met a man."

"Well, sis, it's about time you met a man. You haven't dated anyone since you left the Rat."

"I know. But this might not be the right thing."

Somehow she couldn't bring herself to tell him that the man she was talking about was Ethan Benton. The billionaire vice president, soon to be CEO, of the company Vince worked for.

"So you'll move on to something else. We've done that enough times in our life, haven't we?"

"That we have, bro."

How often had their mother made promises? Then broken them.

"Straight up or fall down!" they recited in unison.

"Get some sleep, Holz. You sound tired."

Holly continued sketching after the call. Line after line, listening to song after song. More glasses of water downed in one go.

Finally she sprawled across the sofa and pondered the painting of Ethan on the wall. His mouth... That urgent mouth that had covered hers a few midnights ago atop the Empire State Building. He had kissed her lips. Along her throat. Behind her ear. Her eyelids.

They fluttered with the memory.

The phone woke her up.

"Hello?" Her voice was gravelly.

"Ethan, here."

"How's Louise?"

"Stable. She was not badly injured by the fall."

"Thank heavens."

Holly's eyes didn't want to open fully. The sound of his voice caressed her, but didn't erase the sting of him banning her from the hospital yesterday. Despite wishing he'd make mention of it, she knew he wouldn't.

She had to carry on forward. "What time is it?"

"Eight in the morning."

Tonight was the gala. Her end of the bargain was due.

"Are you still at the hospital?"

"No, I came back to one of the hotel suites to get some sleep. I did not want to wake you by coming in during the middle of the night."

Holly stroked the leather of the sofa where Ethan had been sleeping the past few nights. If he had come home he'd have found her conked out on it after she simply hadn't been able to stand at the easel any longer.

She'd done eight different renderings of Vince. Must have been some sort of homesickness, she mused to herself now, in the gray haze of the cloudy morning.

She stretched her neck. "What happens now?"

"Aunt Louise will be discharged in a couple of hours. Then I will send Leonard to pick you up. He will help you manage my tuxedo and your gown and whatever else you need. We can get dressed in this suite. I have ordered food. And a makeup artist and hairstylist are coming."

"Okay."

Ethan had everything so organized it made her head spin. How did he keep himself together? She needed a shower and coffee.

"Be prepared for a busy day and night," he continued. "I hope you are ready, my fiancée. Because it is showtime."

When the makeup and hair people departed the hotel suite, Holly and Ethan were finally alone for the first time all afternoon.

The last few hours had flown by. People from Benton Worldwide and from their public relations firm had come and gone from the lavish suite that had a bedroom, living room and dining table in addition to the spacious dressing area where they were now.

All of the suite's Zen-like furnishings and décor were made from precious woods and fine fabrics, while floor-to-ceiling windows provided panoramic views of the Manhattan skyline, where the gloomy and rain-drenched day had turned to dusk.

It had been a whirlwind of introductions as Ethan had presented Holly, although of course he hadn't yet revealed their engagement. Members of the shareholders' board of directors had been in to confer with Ethan. And Holly had finally met Ethan's trusted assistant, Nathan—a young man wielding four electronic devices in his two hands.

A sandwich buffet and barista bar had kept everyone fortified. Then the glam squad had arrived to give Ethan a haircut and work their magic on Holly, before filing out just now to do the same for Louise.

In the first quiet moment since she had arrived, Holly inspected herself in the mirror. She wore a white satin robe, but had already put on her jewelry and heels.

Shimmery eye makeup and soft pink lipstick gave her skin a luminous glow. The style wizards had managed to remove every speck of paint from her cuticles, so that a pearly pink manicure could complement the gown. Her hair was magically doubled in volume, thanks to the expert blow-dry she'd just received.

They had experimented with hairstyles, but gave Ethan veto power. Every time she'd asked his opinion of one of the looks they'd tried he had taken a long gander at her. He'd stopped to scratch his chin, or shot her a wink or half a smile. The way he'd studied every inch of her had been almost obscenely exciting.

And seemingly had had little to do with her hairstyle. Because each time he had decreed that he liked her hair better down.

Now she observed Ethan's reflection behind her in the mirror. He was perched on a stool in the dressing area, reading over some papers, already in tuxedo pants and dress shoes. His stiff white shirt was on, but had not yet been buttoned. She imagined her fingers tracing down the center of his bare, lean chest.

This was really happening. She was in this castle of a hotel, about to be crowned as princess and then ride off on a majestic horse with this regal prince.

Of course in real life at the end of the night they'd shake hands on a con well played. But what the heck? She might as well enjoy it.

"Louise was okay when you talked to her a little while ago?"

"Under the circumstances." Ethan didn't look up from his work.

"I have an idea for tonight that might make it easier on her," Holly said as she tightened one of her earrings in front of the mirror.

"Oh?"

"You were telling me that when it's time for her to give her CEO speech you'll escort her from the table up the stairs to the stage?"

"Yes."

"I was thinking it may be difficult for her to walk up the stairs after her fall. And it won't help to have a thousand people staring at her."

"What is the alternative?"

"I noticed that there is a side entrance to the stage from the waiters' station. While the video montage is playing, and it's dark in the ballroom, we could help Louise get away from the table and up to the stage that way. With no one watching her. Then, when she's introduced, all she has to do is come out from the side of the stage and go to the podium."

Holly followed Ethan's reflection in the mirror as he walked toward her. He came up behind her and circled his arms around her shoulders. He hugged her so authentically, so affectionately, she melted.

"Thank you for thinking of that," he said softly into her ear. "Thank you for thinking about it at all. My, my.... You have already gone far beyond what I expected of you. Please accept my gratitude."

She wanted to tell him how horribly it had hurt when

he hadn't let her go to the hospital yesterday. How much she'd wanted to be part of his family, and not just what her obligations required. How she longed to be there for him in good times and in bad.

She still had so much of her heart left to share. Nothing in her past had squelched that out of her.

But she'd never get to give that heart to him.

Even though she was now positive that he was the only man to whom she ever could.

Fearing she might cry, and tarnish her stellar makeup job, she flicked an internal switch and squirmed away from him.

"Can you help me into my gown? It weighs about ten pounds!"

Ethan went to back to the stool he had been sitting on and patted his tablet for music. A smooth male voice sang a romantic song.

Not taking his eyes off her, he drank a sip from his water bottle and then recapped it. "I would love to help you into your dress."

She raced over and punched into his tablet the upbeat music that she favored.

Ethan's grin swept across his lips.

Holly couldn't resist sashaying her hips to the rhythm as she turned and headed to the closet where her gown hung. She was sure she heard him gasp when she let her robe fall to the floor to reveal the skimpy undergarments underneath.

And so the pretend soon-to-be-married couple helped each other get dressed for the gala.

"Careful with the base of the zipper—it's delicate."

"Blast! Do this right cufflink for me. I am no good at all with my left hand."

"I hope this eye makeup doesn't look too dark in the photos."

"I do not know how women can dance in those heels. I am booking you a foot massage for tomorrow."

"Is my hair perfect?"

"Shoulders back."

"How do I look?"

"How do *I* look?"

The supposed future Mr. and Mrs. Ethan Benton exited the suite preened, perfumed and polished to perfection.

Just as they reached the entrance to the ballroom Ethan remembered he had the engagement ring in his pocket. He skimmed it onto Holly's finger.

Yet again.

They entered the gala to a cacophony of guests, cameras and lights befitting a royal wedding.

CHAPTER ELEVEN

THE BALLROOM VIBRATED with the din of a thousand people. Holly's heart thundered in her chest as Ethan maneuvered them from table to table for introductions. He charmed all the women and the men regarded him with great respect.

"Ethan, how has another year passed already?"

"Lovely to see you, Mrs. Thorpe. Good evening, Mr. Thorpe." Ethan pecked the older lady's cheek and shook the hand of her white-haired husband. "I would like to introduce you to Holly Motta."

Mrs. Thorpe's crinkly eyes lit up. "Well, now, Ethan, are we to believe that you have given up the single life at last?"

"Only because *you* are already spoken for," Ethan said, flattering her.

Holly was dumbstruck and could only squeak out, "Nice to meet you."

She felt horribly out of place. The giddy fun of getting dressed was gone now, and in this moment she felt like a young child in a Halloween princess costume. It was one thing to imagine being the fiancée of a respected and victorious billionaire. But it was another thing entirely actually to be presented as such.

"You look exquisite," Ethan whispered in her ear, as if he sensed her discomfort.

It offered no reassurance.

This wasn't going at all the way she'd thought it would. She hadn't felt this kind of pressure on the yacht the other evening, when Ethan had made small talk with casual acquaintances. The people here tonight knew him well, and she felt as if everyone—but *everyone*—was inspecting her. Panic pricked at her skin like needles, even while her brain told her she must not let Ethan down.

Taking short and fast breaths, she shook hands with a plastered-on smile.

"Henri!" Ethan clasped the shoulder of a mustached man. *"Cela fait longtemps."*

"Ça va?"

"Marie. *Magnifique, comme toujours.*" Ethan kissed the man's wife on both cheeks. *"Je vous présente* Holly Motta."

French. Naturally Ethan spoke perfect French. As men who take showers on private planes were likely to do.

As they walked away he told her, "Mr. and Mrs. Arnaud made a substantial personal donation to a low-income housing project we did outside of Paris."

"Merci!" Holly threw over her shoulder.

Ethan's eyes always took on a special shine when he mentioned those charity projects that were so important to him.

They approached a stone-faced man whose huge muscles were all but bursting out of a tuxedo that was a size too small. He stood ramrod-straight, with his arms folded across his chest. Holly saw that he wore a discreet earpiece with a barely noticeable wire.

"Holly Motta, this is Chip Foley, our head of security," Ethan introduced her.

Chip bent toward Ethan's ear. "I take it you received that fax with the information you requested, sir?"

Ethan looked confused. "No, I did not."

A Japanese couple were coming toward them.

"Ethan. *Ogenki desu ka?*"

The woman wore an elaborate kimono.

"Hai, genki desu," he answered back.

French wasn't intimidating enough. He had to speak Japanese, too.

The evening was starting off like a freezing cold shower.

Holly had imagined it was going to be easier. And more fun. What girl wouldn't want to be at the ball with the dashing prince she was madly in love with?

Madly. In. Love. With.

The four words echoed through her as if someone had yelled them into her ear. Especially the third word. Because there was no denying its truth.

She was in love with this sophisticated, handsome, brilliant man beside her.

Had it happened the very night she'd arrived in New York, when she'd opened the door to the apartment and found him reading his newspaper with that one curl of hair hanging in front of his eyes?

Had it been when he'd bought her all the painting supplies she'd been able to point to, because took her seriously as an artist in a way that no one else ever had?

Maybe it had been atop the Empire State Building, when those earth-shattering kisses had quaked through her like nothing she'd known before?

Or had it been on the yacht, under the tender shadow of the Statue of Liberty, when they'd danced together as one, late into the night?

It didn't matter.

Because she was in love with Ethan Benton.

And that was about the worst thing that had ever happened to her.

"We should make our way to the table now," Ethan said, after finishing his small talk in Japanese.

He took her hand and led them toward the head table, where Aunt Louise and Fernando were already sitting.

Awareness of his touch was a painful reminder that Holly would never have a bona fide seat at this family table. There would be no keeping the glass slippers. The Ethan Bentons of this world didn't marry the Holly Mottas. She was a commoner, hired to do a job—hardly any different from either a scullery maid or an office assistant in his corporation.

Ethan's world was a tightly coiled mechanism of wheels. She was but one small cog. Loving him was going to be *her* problem, not his.

She willed herself not to fall apart now. Overall, Ethan had been kind and generous to her. She had to hold her end up. That much she owed him. Despite the fact that she was crumbling inside.

Love was awful.

"Louise, you look wonderful tonight." Holly greeted the older woman with a kiss on the cheek.

The style magicians had worked wonders. None of the scrapes and bruises from her fall were visible. No one would guess she wore a wig that was thicker and more lustrous than her own thinning hair. Shiny baubles complemented her black gown.

Holly nodded hello to Fernando who, in return, lifted his nose and looked away.

Fernando sat on one side of Louise and Ethan the other. Holly sat next to Ethan. Rounding out their table were company VIPs whom she'd been introduced to earlier today but couldn't remember their names.

As the ballroom's lights were slightly dimmed a spotlight was aimed on Louise, and a waiter brought her a microphone. Louise stood, subtly using the table for leverage and balance. Holly saw a grimace pass quickly across her face.

"Good evening, Benton Worldwide extended family," Louise greeted the guests. "It's been another profitable and productive year for us, which you'll hear about in my report later. As you know my late husband, Melvin Benton, and his brother, Joseph Benton, began this company with the purchase of a one-bedroom apartment in South Boston. And look where we are today."

The ballroom filled with the sound of applause.

"Together we have made this happen. Melvin taught me many things. The most important of which is that money in our wallets means nothing without love in our hearts."

Louise smiled at Ethan and Holly.

"And so," she continued, "if you'll indulge an old woman before we get on to pie charts and growth projections, I'd like to share something personal with you."

A hush swept the room.

"Many of you have watched my nephew Ethan grow up over the decades. I hope you share in my pride at the man he's become. He's a leader who drives himself hard, a savvy negotiator who insists on fairness, and a shrewd businessman with a philanthropic spirit."

The guests applauded again.

Ethan bowed his head, clearly embarrassed by the accolades. Holly touched his arm. He turned his head slightly toward her.

"Yet there's been one thing missing. It has always been my greatest wish for Ethan that he would find a partner to share his life with. To rejoice with in triumph and to weep with in sorrow. To have a home. To have children. To know a love like Mel and I had. And it's with great joy tonight that I announce that Ethan has found that soul mate. And, although it's asking a lot of her to meet her extended family of one thousand all in one evening, I'd like to introduce you to Ethan's fiancée: Miss Holly Motta."

Ethan and Holly looked at each other, both knowing this was their moment. They rose from their chairs in unison and turned to face the crowd. Holly's chest crackled at the irony of the moment.

Applause and good wishes flooded the room.

"Bravo!"

"Bravo!"

"It's about time!"

"Holly!"

"Ethan!"

They smiled and waved on cue—as if they were a royal couple on a palace balcony. Guests began tapping their knives against their water glasses in a signal for a couple to kiss.

Without hesitation, Ethan leaned in to Holly's lips. Thankfully not with a passionate kiss that would have thrown her off balance. But it wasn't a quick peck either. Perhaps he was incapable of a kiss that didn't stir her up inside.

She felt herself blushing. When she giggled a little the guests cheered.

As planned, the chandeliers were dimmed further and the dance floor became bathed in a golden light. Ethan took Holly's hand and brought her to the center of the dance floor, this time as two thousand eyes fixed on them.

The love song from their practice session boomed out of the sound system.

Holly lifted one hand to Ethan's shoulder. One of his fastened around her waist. Their other hands met palm to palm.

They floated across the dance floor, bodies locked, legs in sync. The moment was so perfect Holly wanted to cry.

It was a moment she would never forget. Yet, in time she must learn to forget, if she was ever to love someone who could return her love.

With the gleam of lights beaming down on the dance floor and the rest of the ballroom darker, it was hard to see. Yet Holly's eyes landed on the table where they had been seated. Ethan turned her as they danced, but she kept craning her neck to focus on a strange sight.

Louise was chatting with a couple who had come over to the table. Meanwhile Fernando finished his drink and stood up. He reached into his tuxedo jacket's pocket and pulled out two pieces of paper. He placed one on the chair where Holly was sitting and the other on Ethan's seat. Then he smirked with a satisfied nod.

Holly was so spectacularly beautiful Ethan couldn't help glancing down at her as they danced. She was really just as fetching—if not more so—casual and barefoot in a tee shirt and jeans, having breakfast at the apartment. But tonight... The dance floor lights cast an incandescent glow on her face. The baby pink of her lipstick emphasized the sensual plumpness of her mouth.

It made him want to brand her with kiss after kiss, until he had to hold her up to keep her from falling to the ground. His body reacted—in fact overreacted—to the intimate feel of her breasts, belly and hips pressed to him as he held her close.

Every now and then the sobering fact that Holly wasn't really his fiancée would flit across his mind. There wasn't ever going to be the wedding, home and children that Aunt Louise had spoken of during her toast. He batted away the reality of those thoughts every time they came near. If only for tonight, he actually did want to believe the masquerade was real.

He could risk that much.

Yet a voice in his gut pleaded with him to stop. Told him that he knew better. That his mission had been to guard and defend. That dangerous fantasies would confuse his intentions and lead to irrevocably bad decisions.

Opposing forces argued within him. So his rational

mind welcomed the distraction when he followed Holly's eyes to the table where they'd been sitting. He watched with curiosity as Fernando placed a piece of paper on his and Holly's chairs.

As soon as the dance was over Ethan nodded politely at the applauding guests to the left and to the right. When the next song began he gestured for others to join in the dancing. Couples stood and approached. Once the rhythm was underway, and the dance floor was well populated, he gestured to Holly to return to their table.

Ethan slipped the piece of paper on his chair into his jacket pocket and sat down, trying not to draw any attention to the action. When everyone was occupied with their first-course salads and dinner conversation, he'd discreetly look at it.

Holly held her piece of paper in her lap. She looked downward to read it.

Her face changed instantly. The rosy blush of her cheeks turned ashen white. The blue in her eyes darkened to a flat gray. She blinked back tears.

Trancelike, she slowly stood.

Her murmur was barely audible, and directed to no one in particular. "Excuse me…"

Fortunately, with the dance floor in full swing and one of the video presentations playing on several screens throughout the room, Holly's exit from the table didn't appear too dramatic.

Ethan watched her cross the ballroom as if she was headed to the ladies' lounge.

Instead she opened a sliver of one of the French doors that led to the ballroom's terrace. She slipped through and closed it behind her.

At the table, Ethan caught Fernando's eye. He grinned at Ethan like a Cheshire cat. Ethan's blood began to boil.

But he kept his cool as he rose. He moved slowly toward the terrace. And slid out through the same door Holly had.

The frigid and windy evening slapped across his face and straight under the fabric of his tuxedo. Holly stood across the large plaza of the terrace with her back to him. He figured she must be chilled to the bone.

What was it that had upset her so much that she'd had to leave the ballroom and retreat to this empty space that was not in use during the winter months?

With dread in his heart, Ethan pulled the paper from his pocket.

His temples pulsated louder with each word he read.

Fax to Ethan Benton from Chip Foley, Head of Security, Benton Worldwide Properties.

Regarding Holly Motta.

Per your request, I have gathered the following intelligence.

Holly Motta, age twenty-nine, last known residence Fort Pierce, Florida.

Internet and social media presence significant only as it relates to her occupation as an artist.

No criminal record.

Sometimes known as Holly Dowd.

Married until two years ago to a Ricky Dowd, age twenty-eight, also of Fort Pierce.

Married and divorced.

"Holly!" he spat.

Her shoulders arched at the sound of his voice.

She spun around and they marched toward each other. Meeting in the middle of the grand stone terrace.

"You had me *investigated*?" she accused, rather than questioned.

"You were *married*?" he fired back.

"Without telling me?"

"Without telling me?"

"That must simply be business as usual for you, Mr. Benton. Background checks on the hired help and all that."

"As a matter of fact, it is. My family has spent two generations building our empire. We had better damn well protect it with every tool we have."

"You might have let me know."

The hammering at Ethan's temples threatened to crack open his skull as he read the fax aloud.

"'Ricky Dowd, also known as Rick Dowd and Riff Dowd, indicted for armed robbery at age nineteen. Served twenty-two months in prison, released early due to penitentiary overcrowding. Indicted six months ago, again for armed robbery. Currently serving a sentence at Hansen Correctional Facility in central Florida.'"

Ethan broke away from the page to glare at Holly.

"Twice indicted for armed robbery?"

He felt heat rise through his body in a fury that, for once, he might not be able to contain.

Holly's face was lifeless. Her eyes downcast. She didn't even seem to be breathing.

Finally she muttered softly, "I didn't know Ricky was in prison again."

"But you knew who you married." Ethan's jaw locked.

"The first robbery was before we were married. This new incident happened after our divorce. I haven't seen or talked to him in two years."

"Yet you married a convicted criminal? And deliberately withheld that from me? How will that look to my shareholders? Do you not understand the importance of an impeccable reputation?"

Ethan was approaching cruelty. Rubbing salt into her wounds. But he couldn't stop himself.

Women were never who they seemed! Once again a female had betrayed him. Had not been honest. The same as every other woman he had known. The same as his mother.

This was exactly what he'd been warning himself of, despite his growing attachment to Holly. Why would she turn out to be any different from the others? How dense was he still not to have learned his lesson?

They'd spent so much time together this week. Yet all along she'd withheld the information that not only had she been married, but to someone convicted of serious crimes. She obviously didn't understand how, if that information was to be revealed publicly, it would become an integral part of people's perception of her. Of them.

What else was she hiding? Omission was its own form of lying. And he'd always known that if this engagement façade was to work, they'd have to be straightforward with each other. He'd told her about his future plans for Benton Worldwide. She knew about his aunt's health problems. He'd even let her witness Louise being wheeled out on a stretcher by the paramedics. Without measuring the risks of his actions, he had, in fact, trusted Holly.

Trust. Every year, at every shareholders' gala at this hotel, Ethan got a reminder that *trust* was a dirty word. One that he should never factor into an equation. After all, a boy whose father had just died should have been able to trust that his mother had his best interests at heart.

To read this background information about Holly, to confirm that he didn't know her at all, was an unbearable confusion. Just like the one he'd suffered as a boy, never really knowing his mother, or what could make a woman betray her only child.

A familiar fist pummeled his gut more viciously than ever. He wanted to scream. For the nine-year-old boy who'd lost both his parents within a few months of each other. One in a horrifying car accident.

To complicate matters even more, he was also seething

with jealousy that Holly had given her hand in marriage to another man. *Any* other man! Irrationally, he wanted her only for himself.

Ethan clenched his teeth and read on while Holly clutched her own copy of the fax.

> *Brother Vincent Motta, age twenty-six.*
> *Well-regarded employee at Benton Miami office.*
> *Mother Sally Motta, age forty-eight.*
> *Dozens of jobs, ranging from waitress to telemarketer to factory employee. No position held longer than six months. Never married. Motta appears to be maiden name.*
> *Father of Holly Motta—unknown.*
> *Father of Vincent Motta—unknown.*
> *Unknown whether Holly and Vincent have the same father.*

It was hard to say whose story was sadder—his or Holly's.

Her lower lip trembled uncontrollably until a sob erupted from her throat. "So now you know everything, Mr. Benton!" she cried. "Do you want to share my humiliating past with everyone in the ballroom?"

As tears rolled down her face she shivered in the cold and used both hands to rub at her bare arms.

"I do not know *what* I want to do!" Ethan shouted—uncharacteristically.

He yanked off his tuxedo jacket and wrapped it around her shoulders. "If you had given me all this information at the outset I could have discussed it with my team."

"Discussed it with your team?" She pulled the jacket closer around her. "What would you have done? Created a new identity for me? Erased the past? You masters of the world think of everything, don't you?"

"That is exactly what we have been doing, is it not? We have dressed you up and presented you as a suitable bride for me. Which is what we agreed upon in the beginning."

"Yes. Playing dress-up. Pretending someone like me could be *suitable* for someone like you. My mistake, Ethan. I thought we had become more than our contract. I thought we had…" She eyed the ground again. "I thought we had become friends."

He blamed himself for this predicament. It had been insanity to hire someone he'd only just met for this charade. In fact the whole ruse had been preposterous. Paying someone to pose as his fiancée in order to get Aunt Louise to retire. His heart had been in the right place, but he'd had a temporary lapse in judgment.

In fact he'd been deceitful to Aunt Louise. The one and only woman in his life who had always been truthful with him. Although he knew that no matter how big a mess he'd made of everything his aunt would still love him. That he could depend on.

For one of the only times in his life Ethan didn't know what to do. Didn't know how to reckon with all the events of the past few days. Just as he didn't know where to put the decades of shame that had mixed with the years of phenomenal successes.

And he surely didn't know how to make sense of his feelings for Holly. For once he was out of his league.

After a stare-down with her that had them both turning blue with cold, logic set in.

He wondered aloud, "How did Fernando get this fax from Chip Foley?"

Holly explained how she had seen Fernando take a fax from the machine when they'd had him and Louise over for dinner. Because Fernando used the apartment during his trips to New York, she hadn't thought it unusual that he'd receive a fax there.

"That weasel…" Ethan scowled with disgust.

All along Fernando had been conjuring up ways to ruin Ethan's engagement because he didn't want to move to Barbados with Aunt Louise. He no doubt planned to use Holly's history as a way to prove her an unbefitting bride.

"I will deal with him later. We will sort *all* this out later. For now, we will go back inside and finish the evening as planned."

"Okay," Holly whispered, but it wasn't convincing. She looked utterly shell-shocked with his jacket grasped tightly around her. The rims of her eyes were red and her makeup had smeared.

"I will slip back into the ballroom. You will go up to the suite and pull yourself together. I will meet you back at the table."

"Yes," she consented.

Ethan only hoped she'd be able to get through the rest of the night.

Once inside, Holly handed him his jacket and ducked toward the exit. Ethan soon got roped into a conversation with a Swedish architect. He returned to the table just as the wait staff cleared the salad plates. His and Holly's were untouched.

Ethan made small talk with his tablemates as the main course was served. Over and over again the information in the fax repeated itself in his brain. And he kept glancing in the direction Holly should be returning from. It seemed to be taking her an inordinate amount of time.

Guests were enjoying their surf-and-turf entrées of lobster and filet mignon. A pleasant buzz filled the ballroom.

Still no Holly.

Maybe she'd fallen and hurt herself.

Maybe she'd been taken ill.

Maybe she'd been so upset by the fax that she was crying her eyes out.

Ethan had to go find her. But just as he was about to get up the president of the board of shareholders, Denny Wheton, stood from his seat at the next table. A spotlight landed on him. A waiter gave him a microphone.

"Ladies and gentlemen…" Denny began.

Ethan scanned the whole ballroom for Holly, his insides filling with fear that Denny was going to make a toast to them.

"On behalf of the shareholders' board," Denny continued, confirming Ethan's worry, "I want to express our delight at the news of Ethan's engagement. As Louise said earlier, we've watched Ethan become the driving force of Benton Worldwide. His father and uncle would be proud. As to his bride…we haven't had a chance to get to know her yet, but we're sure Ethan has chosen her with the same diligence and discernment he puts into all his endeavors. To Holly and Ethan! Congratulations!"

Guests at the other tables lifted their glasses.

"Congratulations!"

Voices came from every corner of the room.

Ethan froze as a second spotlight beamed onto him. Hadn't Denny stopped to notice that Holly was not in her seat? He'd probably had too much to drink.

"Holly?" Denny called into his microphone.

The congratulations ceased. The room became silent.

"Holly?"

A microphone was handed to Ethan.

Who had to think fast.

"Thank you for your good wishes," Ethan stated robotically.

He'd kill himself if something bad had happened to her.

"I apologize that Holly is not present for this toast. She is feeling a bit under the weather."

"Under the weather?" Denny boomed into his microphone. "*Under the weather?* Will Benton Worldwide be introducing the next generation's CEO nine months from now?"

The ballroom exploded with applause and cheers.

CHAPTER TWELVE

HOLLY HAD NEVER been so relieved to be home in her entire life. She toed the apartment door closed and leaned back against it. With a deep sigh she dropped the couple of bags she had retrieved from the hotel suite before catching a taxi.

She closed her eyes for a few breaths, hoping to shut out all that had happened.

When she opened them again everything was still the same.

Only she had made matters worse by running away from Ethan and the gala.

En route to the bedroom, she heard her crystal gown swish audibly in the quiet of the apartment. A sound that hadn't been heard under all the activity at the gala. The sky-high heels were killing her, so they were quickly nudged off.

It was a struggle to reach the zipper of her dress. Much nicer earlier tonight, when Ethan had zipped her in. Eventually she was carefully able to wriggle out of the dress. Her impulse was to leave it pooled on the floor, but the adult in her at least managed to put it on the bed.

This gown wasn't her life.

Her jeans and tee shirt were familiar friends.

This wasn't her home.

It was time to go.

Time to cut her losses.

Holly had too much experience with that. Her marriage. Her mother. False hopes and grand promises that hadn't panned out. This was simply another.

With her tail between her legs, it was time to take two steps backward and keep striving for that next step ahead.

Sure, memories of New York would sting. Memories of Ethan would slice deeper than any wounds she'd ever endured before. But she was no stranger to pain.

Besides, she was supposed to be working on herself. Not getting mixed up in someone else's priorities. Not falling in love. This was the wrong road. Time to change direction.

Packing her clothes took less time than she'd thought it would. It was still the middle of the night. With plans to leave in the morning, she paced the apartment.

In the living room, the paper ring Ethan had made from his beer bottle label still sat on the coffee table. The one he'd used to propose to her with. When he had asked her to embark on a business venture that was *not* to become a matter of the heart. For the moment she still wore the enormous diamond that had been on and off her finger all week.

Holly rolled the ring round and round on her finger. She thought about the symbolism of rings—how the circle could never be broken. It had no beginning and it had no end. Continuous. Lasting. Eternal.

Undying love was *not* her and Ethan's story.

Their tale was of two people who had crossed paths in a New York City apartment. Now they both needed to continue on their separate journeys. Ethan built skyscrapers, but was determined not to build love. Holly had a past she could never escape.

His investigation into her hadn't even uncovered all her dirty laundry. He hadn't found out that she wasn't sure if the man who'd shown up every few years while she was growing up was really her father. Despite her mother's insistence that he was.

Wayne had been nice enough to her and Vince when he'd pass through town. He'd take them to get some cheap clothes that he'd pay for with a short fold of twenty-dollar bills he'd pull from his front pants pocket. Then they'd be shuffled off to a neighbor's house so that he could spend time alone with their mother.

Neither Holly nor Vince looked like him. But nor did they look like each other. It wasn't something they talked about much. They couldn't be any closer than they already were. What difference did it make? They could have DNA testing, but it wouldn't matter.

So she had never known whether she and her brother were half or full siblings. Or who their father—or fathers—were. They shared the same eyes as their mother. That was all Holly could be sure of.

Sally's blue eyes had been cloudy and bloodshot the last time Holly had seen her, five years ago.

Vince! Sorrow rained down on her. Her actions—lashing out at Ethan about the investigation and then abruptly leaving the gala without a word to him or to Louise— would cast an unprofessional shadow on Vince.

Her knees buckled and she sank down to the edge of a chair, vowing never to forgive herself if she had ruined her brother's chances at the promotion he'd worked so hard for.

Head in hands, she began to cry for all she and Vince had lacked when they were children. Not just material things, but adults to provide the care that every child needed. As much as they had looked out for each other, they'd always have holes in their hearts.

She wept for this week—for this failed chance to catapult her career to a potential high. For this lost opportunity to turn her goals into reality.

And she sobbed because she'd unexpectedly found a love in Ethan truer than any she could have imagined.

A love that the crux of her knew she would never have again. But she wasn't able to claim it.

Numbly, she picked up her phone. "Vinz…?"

"What's wrong?"

Only her brother would know after one syllable that she was shattered.

With the back of her hand she wiped the tears from her face. "I guess New York is not how I thought it would be."

"You wouldn't be the first person to say that."

"The thing is, I sort of think I've let you down."

Holly stopped herself there. She didn't have to explain everything right now. Maybe Ethan wouldn't hold all this against Vince. At this point she didn't have any control over the situation. All she had was regrets.

"Why would you have let me down? Because you took a shot and it didn't pan out? At least you did it."

"I'm just licking my wounds. I want to come home."

Where was home? She'd given up her dingy apartment in Fort Pierce to pin everything on her future. Neither she nor Vince had any current information on their mother's whereabouts.

"Fly here to Miami. My garage is yours to paint in. And my sofa bed has your name on it. I'll pick you up at the airport."

After the call, Holly took inventory of the mini art studio she'd set up by the window. Methodically she cleaned brushes. Tucked sketches into portfolios. She organized neatly, remembering the open tube of paint that had started this magical ride in New York. Cobalt Two Eleven all over her face.

Her gaze darted to the blue-painted sketch of Ethan on the wall. She was so proud of that piece—felt that she had caught his spirit in each line. Power and gravity and sensuality, with demons fighting behind his eyes.

As a matter of fact she would take the painting with her. It would either be a testament to the legacy Ethan would hold in her heart forever. Or it would be a torment that would haunt her for the rest of her days. Either way, it was hers and she wanted it.

With a small knife she found in the kitchen she carefully removed the staples attaching the canvas to its frame. She'd roll up the painting and buy a tube to transport it in before she left town.

There was nothing more to do.

She wasn't interested in sleeping. Didn't want to give up even one last minute of this magical city and its hex that made people believe dreams could come true. These moments were all she had, and she'd treasure them for a lifetime.

She stared out the window. A million stories were unfolding in the city. Hers would end here.

Inching off the diamond engagement ring, she placed it next to the paper ring on the coffee table. Beside each other they were as odd a couple as she and Ethan.

As usual, not knowing what else to do with her feelings, Holly said goodbye to her fancy manicure and reached for her charcoals.

Ethan closed the door on the hotel room where he'd managed a few hours of tortured sleep in a chair. He walked down the hall to Aunt Louise's suite. Still in his tuxedo pants, although his tie was off and the first two buttons of his shirt were undone, he scratched his beard stubble. He'd been unable to face a shower just yet, and had promised his aunt they'd reconvene their discussion during breakfast.

"Come in, Ethan," Louise called out as soon as she heard the keycard click to unlock the door.

"I have not had coffee!" Ethan managed a trace of a smile for his beloved aunt.

"I'll pour you a cup." Louise wore a dressing gown and slippers. She sat at the dining table in her luxury suite, heavy drapes open to the city.

Ethan took the seat across from her.

"Does anything look different to you in the light of morning?" She tipped her eyebrow to him in a familiar way.

When he was a teenager, living with her and Uncle Mel, if he'd been grappling with a dilemma or regretting a bad choice, Aunt Louise would always tell him to sleep on it and see if a new day brought any fresh insight.

The insistence in her arched brow today told him that she had decided what realization he should have come to. His intuition told him what her conclusion was. He peered into his coffee cup to try to shut the thought down.

Something like a tribal drum pounded inside him, urging him to lift his eyes and embrace the truth.

"Where is Fernando?" Ethan tried to change the subject—at least for a moment.

But on and on the internal drum sounded.

"Gone. Good riddance," Louise clipped. "Before dawn this morning I called Bob Parcell to draw up a non-disclosure agreement."

Ethan snorted. "Lawyers work around the clock."

"Ours do. I signed a generous check, contingent on the fact that Fernando never speaks a word about our family, our company or anything to do with us. If he does, our people will make sure the rest of his life is spent behind bars."

"Well done."

Louise took a sip of her coffee, then smacked the cup loudly back onto the saucer. "And *that*, my dear nephew, is the end of my foray into having a younger companion."

After Holly had disappeared last night he and Louise

had held their heads high until the last guest had left the gala. Then they'd sat up together until the wee hours. He'd confessed about the engagement ploy and his motivation behind it. Begged for her forgiveness. Told her about the fax and Fernando's part in it.

Now Ethan lifted his aunt's hand and gently kissed the back of it. "I am so sorry you fell prey to him"

"Don't you think I knew what he was doing?" she retorted. "His trips down here to New York while I stayed in Boston. The restaurant bills that were surely more expensive than dinner for one. Charges to women's clothing shops although I never received any gifts. Fernando was clearly taking advantage of me from the beginning."

"You never told me."

"The vanity of a rich old woman... Perhaps I thought I could simply buy myself something to replace the emptiness left by your Uncle Mel's death. But even with all the money in the world you can't purchase or declare love. You can't arrange it. It's love that rearranges *you*."

Ethan knew what she was telling him. The drum beat louder in his ears. Yet he couldn't. Mustn't. Wouldn't.

"I know that you're torn inside..." Louise continued.

For all her health problems, when Louise Benton was clearheaded she was a shrewd and intelligent woman.

"It's what I feared for you. That after so much loss you wouldn't be able to love. When your mother went—"

"You were the only mother I ever had," Ethan interrupted, taking her hand again. "Everything I have achieved is because of you."

Louise's eyes welled. "I must have done something right. You're a rare man to go through all this trouble to get me to retire. When I said I wanted you to be married and settled before you took over, I never imagined you'd concoct such an elaborate scheme just because I've been too hardheaded to see that my time has come. And I had no idea I'd raised such a skilled imposter!"

She snickered, forcing a crack through Ethan's tight lips.

"We Bentons do what we have to, do we not?" he joked in a hushed voice.

"My guess is that your playacting became real and you've fallen in love with Holly. Am I right, Ethan?"

He wanted to cover his ears, like a young child who didn't want to hear what was being said. *Love* her? Those drumbeats inside him sped up like a jungle warrior charging toward his most threatening battle.

Yes, he loved Holly. He loved her completely—like nothing he'd ever loved before. He wanted to give her everything she'd never had. Wanted to have children with her. Wanted to spend every minute of his life with her. Wanted to hold her forever as both his wife and his best friend.

That invisible opponent marched toward him and pushed him back behind the battle lines.

He lashed out without thinking. "Holly deceived me about her past. She lied to me. Look at what she came from."

"Oh, hogwash!" Louise dismissed. "How about what *you* came from? What *I* came from? Your father and Uncle Mel were brought up on the tough streets of South Boston without a dime or a university degree between them. I was a poor Southie girl whose father skinned fish for a living. It's not shame about Holly's past that you're concerned with. The time has come for you to let go of shame about your own."

Of course he wore shame—like a suit of armor. Who wouldn't be ashamed that his own mother didn't want him?

He studied his aunt's face. Hard-earned wrinkles told the story of a life embraced. Could he let go of his pain and open up to the fullness the world had to offer?

Could he gamble again on trust?

Gamble on Holly?

On himself?

In an instant he knew that if he didn't now, he never would.

He sprang to his feet. Leaned down to Louise and kissed both her cheeks. Moved to the office desk in the well-appointed suite. Wrote a quick note and then sent it through the fax machine.

"Wish me luck," he said as he flew out the door, too impatient to wait for a response.

In his hotel room, he shaved and showered. Called Leonard to bring the car around. He placed a second call to George Alvarez, manager of the Miami office.

"What are your thoughts about the site supervisor position?" Ethan asked him.

Liz Washington, the previous supervisor, had transferred to the Houston office.

"I've had a young guy apprenticing with Liz for a couple of years now. Done a terrific job," George pitched. "He's ready for the step up. Name of Vince Motta."

"Yes, Vince Motta," Ethan approved with relief.

He valued George, and wouldn't want to go against his expertise. But he knew that if he was able to help Vince it would mean a lot to Holly. That was the kind of sister she was. The kind of woman she was.

The kind of woman he was going to make his.

He raced down the hotel corridor to the elevators, and then out through the front entrance of the hotel. Because once Ethan Benton had made up his mind about something, it couldn't happen fast enough.

"To the apartment," he instructed Leonard as he got into the car.

After Holly had vanished from the gala last night Ethan had checked the hotel suites. She had been nowhere to be found. Even though there had been no answer on her cell phone, or at the apartment, that was where he figured she'd gone. A midnight phone call to the building's doorman had confirmed that Holly had indeed arrived by taxi.

Yes, he had called the doorman to investigate her whereabouts! How could she blame him for an action like that? He oversaw a corporation with thousands of employees all over the world. He couldn't possibly command that without being on top of all available knowledge. Information was power. Artistic Holly Motta might not understand that, but he relied on it. She'd have to get used to the way he thought.

Just as he'd have to get used to her freewheeling ways. How she slammed doors closed with one foot. Ordered pizza with everything but the kitchen sink on it. Said whatever came into her mind. Needed to devote hours of scrubbing to getting her hands clean of paint. Ethan thought he wouldn't mind spending a lifetime looking at and holding those graceful fingers that brought art and beauty into the world. Seeing the ring on her finger that proclaimed her lo—

"Leonard! I need to make a stop first. Take me to Fifth and Fifty-Seventh."

Holly winced when she heard the key in the door. If only she'd stuck to her original plan and left at the crack of dawn after her sleepless night. She'd known that Ethan would make his way back here to the apartment. It would have been easier to slink away than to say goodbye in person. What was it that had kept her from going?

Her heart dropped in freefall to the floor as he strode through the door. She wanted to run to him. To put her arms around him. To kiss him until all the problems of the world faded away and there was just the two of them.

"Why did you leave last night?"

His eyes looked weary. His cheeks were flushed.

That one perfect curl of hair that always fell forward on his forehead was dotted with snowflakes. So was his coat.

Holly shifted her gaze out the window to see that it had started to snow. The whole week she'd been in New York it had rained and been cold and dreary. But it hadn't snowed.

She'd fantasized about walking the city streets during a snowfall. Seeing the soft powder billowing down as she crossed busy intersections and marveled at architectural landmarks that stood proudly dusted with white.

Instead she'd be returning to the sunny Florida winter. Snow—*ha!* That was what fantasy was. By definition not real.

"Answer my question," he insisted.

Holly's voice came out hoarse. "I'm truly embarrassed by my behavior. I know it was completely unprofessional."

She cut her eyes toward the floor.

"Look at me. How about the fact that I was worried about you?"

"What do *you* care? Let's be honest."

He stepped in and took her chin in his hand, lifting her face to meet his. "Certainly you leaving the gala without a word was not good business..." he began.

"I'm so sorry."

"But this is not business anymore, and if you want to be honest you know that."

"Know what?"

He moved his hand to caress her cheek tenderly, sending warmth across her skin.

"I love you, Holly. I *love* you. And I suspect you love me, too."

Tears pooled somewhere far behind her eyes. She fought them before saying what she needed to. "Now that you know the truth about me from your investigation, you've found out that I'm not who you want. I'm not a match for you. I'm damaged goods."

"You think you are the only one?"

"What do you mean?"

He let the hand that was touching her face fall to his side. His mouth set in a straight line.

"After my father died…" he started, but then let the words dangle in the air for a minute.

Holly anxiously awaited what he was so hesitant to say.

"Within a few months of my father dying, my mother—who was not much of a mother to begin with—met a man. And together they came up with an idea."

Bare pain burned in Ethan's eyes. Holly knew he was going to tell her something he had to dig out from the rock bottom of his core, where he kept it submerged.

"My mother told Uncle Mel and Aunt Louise that she and this man were going to take me away. That they would never see or hear from me again unless…"

He swallowed hard, his breath rasping and broken.

He regained his voice, "Unless *they* wanted to keep me instead. Which she would allow them to do in exchange for five hundred thousand dollars. In cash. She specified cash."

Agony poured from every cell in Holly's body. Grief for the little boy Ethan. And for herself. For her brother, Vince. For all the children unlucky enough to be born to parents who didn't give them the devotion they deserved.

"So, you see, my mother sold me to my aunt and uncle. I believe that means that you are not the only package of damaged goods around here."

The spoken words swirled around the room.

Again Holly wanted to hug the man she loved.

And again she didn't.

It was time for her to go.

He thought he loved her. He'd fallen for the drama they were starring in.

She'd have to have the cooler head. If she let him believe he loved her, one day he'd wake up and realize that he didn't want something this raw. That instead he could stuff his hurt right back down and act in a different play, with another kind of woman. With someone who'd never have to know about the betrayed and discarded child. About the gashes that still bled, the sores that would never heal. In his next pantomime he could be with a woman who knew only the functional and successful adult he'd managed to become.

She averted her eyes to the diamond ring on the table. To the beer wrapper ring beside it. She bent down for them and handed both to Ethan.

"I am glad you've returned these rings," he said. "They do not belong on your finger."

His words confirmed what she already knew. That it was time to leave.

He reached in his pocket and pulled out a small turquoise box. Holly's breath quickened.

He knelt down on one knee and held it out to her in the palm of his hand.

"Because an ordinary diamond ring does not fit the uniqueness of you. Like this, you are one of a kind."

He opened the box. Inside was the blue topaz ring she had admired from the private gemstone collection they'd seen that day they had gone shopping.

Uncontainable tears rolled down Holly's cheeks.

"I love you, Holly. I have loved you since you bounced through the door with that ridiculous blue paint on your face. I have never met anyone like you. Pretending to be engaged to you has shown me something I never thought I could see."

"What?" Holly asked, her spirits soaring.

"That our pain does not have to define us. That a past and a future can coexist. That there is beauty to be had every day. I want to share those miracles with you. To walk through life together. Please. *Please.* Will you marry me? This time the ring will never leave your finger."

She had to take the chance if he was willing to. To trust their authentic selves—scars and all. Together.

"I will." She nodded as he fitted the ring onto her finger.

Ethan stood. Holly reached her arms up around his neck and drew him into a kiss that couldn't wait a second longer.

Many minutes later he whispered, "Did you check the fax machine?"

"No." She'd heard the sounds and beeps of the machine before he arrived, but she hadn't looked to see what had come. She'd had quite enough of faxes already.

"Go," he prodded.

The piece of paper contained a two-word question.

Will you?

Had she read it earlier, she'd have known he was coming to propose.

She flirted with her fiancé. "Will I…?"

The smile kicked at the corner of his mouth. "Will you teach me how to draw?"

"It's a deal." Her grin joined his.

They pressed their lips to each other's in an ironclad merger, valid for eternity.

* * * * *

*If you loved Andrea's debut book and want to
indulge in more feel-good billionaire romances,
then make sure you try*
THE BILLIONAIRE'S CLUB *trilogy
by Rebecca Winters*

*RETURN OF HER ITALIAN DUKE
BOUND TO HER GREEK BILLIONAIRE
Available now!*

*The last book in the trilogy,
WHISKED AWAY BY HER SICILIAN BOSS,
is out next month!*

MILLS & BOON®
Hardback – September 2017

ROMANCE

The Tycoon's Outrageous Proposal	Miranda Lee
Cipriani's Innocent Captive	Cathy Williams
Claiming His One-Night Baby	Michelle Smart
At the Ruthless Billionaire's Command	Carole Mortimer
Engaged for Her Enemy's Heir	Kate Hewitt
His Drakon Runaway Bride	Tara Pammi
The Throne He Must Take	Chantelle Shaw
The Italian's Virgin Acquisition	Michelle Conder
A Proposal from the Crown Prince	Jessica Gilmore
Sarah and the Secret Sheikh	Michelle Douglas
Conveniently Engaged to the Boss	Ellie Darkins
Her New York Billionaire	Andrea Bolter
The Doctor's Forbidden Temptation	Tina Beckett
From Passion to Pregnancy	Tina Beckett
The Midwife's Longed-For Baby	Caroline Anderson
One Night That Changed Her Life	Emily Forbes
The Prince's Cinderella Bride	Amalie Berlin
Bride for the Single Dad	Jennifer Taylor
A Family for the Billionaire	Dani Wade
Taking Home the Tycoon	Catherine Mann

MILLS & BOON®
Large Print – September 2017

ROMANCE

The Sheikh's Bought Wife	Sharon Kendrick
The Innocent's Shameful Secret	Sara Craven
The Magnate's Tempestuous Marriage	Miranda Lee
The Forced Bride of Alazar	Kate Hewitt
Bound by the Sultan's Baby	Carol Marinelli
Blackmailed Down the Aisle	Louise Fuller
Di Marcello's Secret Son	Rachael Thomas
Conveniently Wed to the Greek	Kandy Shepherd
His Shy Cinderella	Kate Hardy
Falling for the Rebel Princess	Ellie Darkins
Claimed by the Wealthy Magnate	Nina Milne

HISTORICAL

The Secret Marriage Pact	Georgie Lee
A Warriner to Protect Her	Virginia Heath
Claiming His Defiant Miss	Bronwyn Scott
Rumours at Court (Rumors at Court)	Blythe Gifford
The Duke's Unexpected Bride	Lara Temple

MEDICAL

Their Secret Royal Baby	Carol Marinelli
Her Hot Highland Doc	Annie O'Neil
His Pregnant Royal Bride	Amy Ruttan
Baby Surprise for the Doctor Prince	Robin Gianna
Resisting Her Army Doc Rival	Sue MacKay
A Month to Marry the Midwife	Fiona McArthur

MILLS & BOON®
Hardback – October 2017

ROMANCE

Claimed for the Leonelli Legacy	Lynne Graham
The Italian's Pregnant Prisoner	Maisey Yates
Buying His Bride of Convenience	Michelle Smart
The Tycoon's Marriage Deal	Melanie Milburne
Undone by the Billionaire Duke	Caitlin Crews
His Majesty's Temporary Bride	Annie West
Bound by the Millionaire's Ring	Dani Collins
The Virgin's Shock Baby	Heidi Rice
Whisked Away by Her Sicilian Boss	Rebecca Winters
The Sheikh's Pregnant Bride	Jessica Gilmore
A Proposal from the Italian Count	Lucy Gordon
Claiming His Secret Royal Heir	Nina Milne
Sleigh Ride with the Single Dad	Alison Roberts
A Firefighter in Her Stocking	Janice Lynn
A Christmas Miracle	Amy Andrews
Reunited with Her Surgeon Prince	Marion Lennox
Falling for Her Fake Fiancé	Sue MacKay
The Family She's Longed For	Lucy Clark
Billionaire Boss, Holiday Baby	Janice Maynard
Billionaire's Baby Bind	Katherine Garbera